THE BRUISER

Jim Tully, 1886–1947

THE BRUISER

by
JIM TULLY

Edited by Paul J. Bauer and Mark Dawidziak
Foreword by Gerald Early

Black Squirrel Books
KENT, OHIO

Library of Congress Catalog Card Number 2010008636
ISBN 978-1-60635-056-0
Manufactured in the United States of America

First published by Greenberg, New York, 1936.

Library of Congress Cataloging-in-Publication Data
Tully, Jim.
The bruiser / by Jim Tully ; foreword by Gerald Early.
p. cm.
"Edited by Paul J. Bauer and Mark Dawidziak."
ISBN 978-1-60635-056-0 (pbk. : alk. paper) ∞
I. Early, Gerald Lyn.
II. Title.
PS3539.U44B78 2010
813'.52—dc22

2010008636

British Library Cataloging-in-Publication data are available.
14 13 12 11 10   5 4 3 2 1

TO

MY FELLOW

ROAD-KID

JACK DEMPSEY

FOREWORD
by Gerald Early

It's a rough world, Shane—as warm as the very devil
when the referee's raisin' your hand, and cold as a hangman's heart when he ain't.
> —Silent Tim speaking to his fighter,
> Shane Rory, in Jim Tully's *The Bruiser*

Baseball may have captured America's heart, but boxing is
America's body and its soul.

American authors have written a number of noted,
even outstanding, baseball novels including Mark Harris's
quartet, *The Southpaw, Bang the Drum Slowly, A Ticket for
Seamstitch,* and *It Looked like For Ever,* Robert Coover's *The
Universal Baseball Association, Inc., J. Henry Waugh, Prop,*
Bernard Malamud's *The Natural,* W. P. Kinsella's *Shoeless
Joe,* Ring Lardner's *You Know Me, Al,* and Philip Roth's
The Great American Novel. Comparatively speaking, there
have been far fewer great American boxing novels: Budd
Schulberg's *The Harder They Fall,* W. C. Heinz's *The Profes-
sional,* Leonard Gardner's *Fat City,* and F. X. Toole's *Rope
Burns,* which is actually a collection of stories, come im-
mediately to mind. On this short list should be placed the
book you hold in your hands, Jim Tully's neglected novel,
The Bruiser, published in 1936. I shall say more about Tully's
work momentarily.

The fact that more impressive baseball novels than boxing novels have been written cannot be accounted for by the fact that baseball is the more popular sport, so it would be expected to have produced a greater number of novels. That is certainly true today that baseball is more popular, but throughout most of the twentieth century, in the United States, prizefighting, as professional boxing was often called, had a huge and passionate following, million-dollar gates, and huge television contracts. (Indeed, boxing was the first sport to hit television, when the device became available for mass use in the late 1940s, and was televised much more than baseball.) Many heavyweight champions were among not only the most famous athletes of their era but among the most famous celebrities or public figures anywhere. John L. Sullivan, Jack Johnson, Jack Dempsey, Joe Louis, Rocky Marciano, Muhammad Ali, Joe Frazier, and Mike Tyson were among the most famous people on the planet during their heyday, the princes of popular culture. And some fighters in lighter weight divisions were also world-famous: Sugar Ray Robinson, Willie Pep, Henry Armstrong, Emile Griffith, Benny Leonard, Rocky Graziano, Marvelous Marvin Hagler, Sugar Ray Leonard, Alexis Arguello, Roberto Duran, Tommy Hearns, Carlos Monzon, Nino Benvenuti, and Oscar De La Hoya to name only a few. Nearly all of these men made fabulous amounts of money during their careers—whether they were capable of keeping what they earned is another story and some, most famously Louis, Duran, Tyson, and Armstrong wound up broke—and their fights generated enormous publicity, front page in the sports section, sometimes front page news stories.

Highly gifted boxers, regardless of whether they are especially articulate men, are charismatic by virtue of the unsettling but striking combination of naked brutality and muscular yet lissome grace that characterizes their sport. Boxing is the only sport where the object is to break your opponent's will by physically beating him into submission: either to knock him unconscious or to make him quit or make the referee or your opponent's corner make him quit by stopping the fight. The risk the prizefighter takes seems by turns heroic, curious, thrilling, decadent, primitive, or simply absurd. So what if you win? But the same can be said for any sport. Perhaps that is the point of sports, the irrationality of its imbalance: so much is harnessed and expended to prove so little. Its aim is pointless, which is why, perhaps, it is so fascinating, especially to the bourgeoisie who often seem obsessed completely by the need for safety and comfort, the avoidance of risk or any sort of danger. Sometimes absurd risk can be honorable. For no matter how much money a successful boxer makes, no fighter fights only for money. And most fighters do not make much money, in the end, because most never become champion or anything close to it. There is a certain code that drives these men (and now the women who box as well). This point may seem counterintuitive for a sport that is often accused of being faked, fixed, and corrupted by organized crime. Yet boxing has been able to transcend its shoddy origins and debased tendencies, and some boxers have become authentic national heroes. Prizefighting is both the height of inhumanity—to beat another human being senseless if you can—and the essence of what it means to be an exemplary human being—to stand up alone to a fearsome adversary and not be afraid.

American novelist, journalist, socialist reformer, and boxing fan Jack London published what is, by all accounts, the first fictional American boxing story, *The Abysmal Brute,* in book form in 1913 (it had been serialized in 1911); its similarities to Edgar Rice Burroughs' *Tarzan of the Apes* (serialized in 1912), published in book form in 1914, is startling. Both are essentially pulp novels about physically imposing white heroes—Young Pat Glendon and Lord Greystoke, who seem uncivilized—one reared in the woods and mountains and the other reared by apes in the jungle—but in fact are cultured but also more than a match for any man or beast. The love interests in the book, the rich heiress and enterprising journalist Maud Sangster and the intrepid Jane Porter—innocent, young, beautiful but assertive white women (the New Woman of the twentieth century that pundits and arbiters talked about)—are basically the same woman, seeking an extraordinary man to whom they can submit sexually. What both fantasies reflect are the racial phobias about masculinity that troubled the imagination of white America during the reign of the first black heavyweight champion Jack Johnson (1908–1915). The books were serialized during the height of Johnson-mania, right after his much-publicized fight with Jim Jeffries in July 1910, which Johnson won by knockout and which produced racial violence throughout the country, and during his closely followed trial for violation of the White Slavery Act.

The heavyweight champion, at this time, was not only the most famous, toughest *man* in the United States, usually, but he was the most famous, most mythical *male*. The fact that a man from a so-called inferior race beat white men in the ring and became the champion (until the rise of Johnson, white heavyweight champions drew the color line and refused to fight black challengers) was a cause of considerable cultural and social unrest in the United States. Johnson made headlines not only because of his fights against white champions but also because of his affairs and marriages to white women at a time when miscegenation, at least between a black man and a white woman, was outlawed in virtually the entire south, and was a rigidly observed taboo nearly everywhere. Johnson was prosecuted and convicted under the new federal antiprostitution legislation called the Mann Act and sentenced to prison for one year. He fled the country in 1912 to avoid imprisonment and did not serve the sentence until his return to the United States after World War I, at which time he was no longer the heavyweight champion.

But the novels by London and Burroughs also reflect the concern that white men were becoming too civilized, too softened by civilization. The books depicted their white heroes as idealized children of nature, Adamic, Wordsworthian, and rigidly Victorian in their morals; they are, in most respects, prelapsarian man, a form of cultural innocence. The heroes are also strikingly well read, extraordinarily literate. (Amazingly, London's hero prefigures Gene Tunney, who was to defeat Jack Dempsey twice, in 1926 and 1927, marry an heiress, and lecture about Shakespeare in an English class at Yale. Life does on occasion imitate fiction.) Both novels display distrust of civilization; London's novel, for instance, condemns the business of boxing but not the actual performance of the sport, which, ideally, is pure and manly. Cities are seductive, deceptive fleshpots; journalism is a racket.

I mention both Burroughs and particularly London at length because Tully's *The Bruiser* makes use of many of the elements to be found in the earlier novels but tends to turn them on their head or to recast them in a more nuanced, complex way. The rising young fighter of 1936, the year *The Bruiser* was published, was Joe Louis of Detroit, the first black heavyweight to contest seriously for the title since Jack Johnson's defeat at the hands of Jess Willard in Havana in 1915. Louis was not to win the title until 1937 when he defeated Jim Braddock, the Cinderella Man, in eight rounds. But in 1936 Louis lost for the first time in his career when he was pummeled for twelve rounds by Max Schmeling. This defeat set up the rematch in 1938 that became one of the biggest, most anticipated fights of the twentieth century. In the novel, the character Tiger Jones does not quite represent Louis but rather a composite of black fighters (a bit of Louis, a bit of Tiger Flowers, a bit of Joe Walcott, a bit of Henry Armstrong) but certainly the racist but oddly admiring way that the journalist Hot and Cold Daily describes Jones in print is exactly the way Louis was described in the pre-1938 portion of his career, when the white sporting public was more unsure of him and had not taken him to its heart the way it would especially during World War II. In short, the entire atmosphere of both boxing and the United States was different in 1936 from 1911. The 1930s was the era of the Great Depression. Americans saw their country differently; politically, there was a far less pronounced jingoism, less brawny white Anglo-Saxonism. *The Bruiser* is less pulp fiction, although of course pulp fiction has largely an urban working-class audience, than something like a proletarian or working-class novel. In a word, Tully was a hard-boiled fictionist. *The Abysmal Brute* was not quite a novel of the underground, in much the way that a novel by Horatio Alger, despite its aspects of social realism, is not, as the moral sentimentalism makes its less a protest book than an aspiration narrative. *The Bruiser* is a novel of the underground. The characters we are supposed to like are not too good to be true or too superior to their surroundings.

Tully's novel tells the story of Shane Rory, an itinerant fighter, who rides the rods and fights smokers, and his rise to a heavyweight championship fight (the climax of the novel). We learn from the novel, as Shane's manager Silent Tim informs us, "that guiding a man to a heavyweight championship was more delicate than assembling a watch." All the clichés of the boxing novel are here: the hero is an innocent but unlike London's hero, Shane is no intellectual, although one fighter, Bangor Lang, tells him to take up reading to relax. Shane takes up reading for a time while his broken jaw mends, but he does not become an autodidact like Tully, his creator. He suffers something like a failure of nerve in the ring after he sees a punch-drunk fighter, Jerry Wayne, in an asylum and indeed, for a time quits the profession. His mother dies after being pushed from a streetcar by a drunken conductor; his father dies while returning from Panama; his sister dies from consumption. "I had to take it," Shane tells his girlfriend, Lyndal Lund, "It's funny—I don't know why—nobody ever thinks a boy has any troubles—but he has—plenty." He becomes a fighter while hanging around a gym running errands for the boxers. He gets drunk, loses his money more than once, and hangs around with prostitutes like Dilly Dally who take advantage of him; he knowingly and unknowingly participates in fixed fights. But he possesses a moral character: he is the only white man in the entire book who isn't racist; he believes in his ability despite his doubts about his profession; he does not really care about money or taking advantage of people.

In the novel, there is the "good" girl, Lyndal, who lives on a farm and gives up a professor for Shane, and there is the "bad" girl, Berniece Burue, an entertainer who thinks she might be good for Shane. Silent Tim, Shane's manager, is the typical teacher and cynic that one finds in novels of this sort. (Boxing novels, like sports novels generally, are basically "student/teacher" books, usually about the relationship between a younger and an older, more experienced man.) And there is an assorted lot of pugilists whose lives straddle being highly trained craftsmen (there is much about the technique of boxing in this book) and aimless hoboes.

While one can see elements of the life of heavyweight Jack Dempsey in the character of Shane Rory, *The Bruiser* is largely based on Tully's own experiences. Tully was born in Ohio in 1886, the son of a "drunken ditch digger," as Tully describes his father, and his wife. After his mother died, he was placed in an orphanage. By fourteen, he was on his own, tramping from town to town, riding the rods or sneaking in boxcars with other hoboes. He worked in a circus, as a dishwasher, a newspaper boy, a common laborer. He also spent time in jail. In his early twenties, he became a professional featherweight boxer. When he was knocked unconscious, he quit, despite the fact that he showed much promise. Clearly, his depictions of boxing were drawn from his time in the ring, which may be why they have such a ring of authenticity to them, particularly his descriptions of being knocked out or hurt in the ring. So were his descriptions in *The Bruiser* of riding the rails as a hobo.

Tully eventually wound up in Hollywood, working for Charlie Chaplin, and then entering journalism as a magazine writer, revealing the secrets of the movie stars. He also wrote dialogue for movies. At the same time Tully became a novelist and memoirist, unschooled though he was in the craft of novel writing or even in the mechanics of writing English, as he had not finished the equivalent of middle school. He had learned about life with hoboes, life in jail, life in the circus, life on the road. (His descriptions of journalism in *The Bruiser*, indeed, his characterization of the crusty sportswriter Hot and Cold Daily, are worth the price of the book.) He was the precursor of Kerouac, and the America Tully conjured up was a cross between the sensibilities of Walt Whitman and his generative America and Dashiell Hammett and his corrupt America, light and darkness, expansiveness and confinement. Few novelists captured the contradictions of his country so simply or so honestly in the metaphor of the pure, fatalistic, and merciless community of bruising. His work deserves to be rediscovered.

INTRODUCTION

Paul J. Bauer and Mark Dawidziak

Jim Tully (June 3, 1886–June 22, 1947) was an American writer who won critical acclaim and commercial success in the 1920s and 30s. His rags-to-riches career may qualify him as the greatest long shot in American literature. Born near St. Marys, Ohio, to an Irish immigrant ditch-digger and his wife, Tully enjoyed a relatively happy but impoverished childhood until the death of his mother in 1892. Unable to care for him, his father sent him to an orphanage in Cincinnati. He remained there for six lonely and miserable years. What further education he acquired came in the hobo camps, boxcars, railroad yards, and public libraries scattered across the country. Finally, weary of the road, he arrived in Kent, Ohio, where he worked as a chainmaker, professional boxer, and tree surgeon. He also began to write, mostly poetry, which was published in the area newspapers.

Tully moved to Hollywood in 1912, when he began writing in earnest. His literary career took two distinct paths. He became one of the first reporters to cover Hollywood. As a freelancer, he was not constrained by the studios and wrote about Hollywood celebrities (including Charlie Chaplin, for whom he had worked) in ways that they did not always find agreeable. For these pieces, rather tame by current standards, he became known as the most-feared man in Hollywood—a title he relished. Less lucrative, but closer to his heart, were the books he wrote about his life on the road and the American underclass. He also wrote an affectionate memoir of his childhood with his extended Irish family, as well as novels on prostitution and Hollywood and a travel book. While some of the more graphic books ran afoul of the censors, they were also embraced by critics, including H. L. Mencken, George Jean Nathan, and Rupert Hughes. Tully, Hughes wrote, "has fathered the school of hard-boiled writing so zealously cultivated by Ernest Hemingway and lesser luminaries."

Few Americans saw more of their country than Jim Tully. During his road years, 1901–1907, that view of everything from farms in Ohio and wheat fields in Nebraska to small towns in Mississippi and sprawling California orchards flashed by, usually framed by the steel sides of an open boxcar door. But there was another, less bucolic America of hobo jungles, railroad yards, and back alleys. And it was this America that young Tully called home. And a boy who lived in *that* America depended on his wits and, sometimes, his fists. After half-a-dozen years, he'd had enough. It was time to try life as a citizen. He left the road much as he'd begun: tentative and unsure of where he wanted to go. He'd first worked at a chain factory in St. Marys, and his only real plan when he arrived in Kent, Ohio, was to make his way to the chain factory and secure employment working hot links, the one job for which he might reasonably claim experience. Making chain would be a start, but he wanted more.

He possessed few other skills that would gain him admission to 9–5 life. Having little formal education and being the son of Irish immigrant parents didn't afford him the option of working in daddy's firm or marrying the banker's daughter and being installed a vice president. Instead, he chose a path favored by immigrants and drifters. He would put on boxing gloves and enter the ring.

Tully's boxing training amounted to little more than sparring in a gym. As he later recalled in the third-person,

> Environment seemed bound to make him a pugilist. He fought so many brakemen, yeggs, and railroad detectives (he lumps them altogether) that he subconsciously became a trained fighter. Drinking rotgut whiskey, he battled galore in box cars and saloons. He learned the elemental lesson of the survival of the fittest. For in tramp life the struggle is primal and the weak are used as door mats while the strong are respected.

It would be, if nothing else, (mostly) honest money.

Tully had met other boxers, past, present, and future, in his travels. And as he embarked on his new profession, he recalled the advice he'd been given by one of them. The great lightweight champion, Joe Gans, advised Tully: "Don't pay any attention to the fellow you fight—just act like he's not in the world." It proved difficult advice to follow for one without Gans's skills, and Tully's ring career never came close to that of the black legend. Still, for the next several years, Tully earned at least part of his living in the ring. His journeyman ring career ended in San Francisco in 1912.

> It was in the fourth round—I learned later.
> A right caught me. I was unconscious until the next afternoon.

All events which preceded the fight, and everything which happened in the ring has been in eclipse all these years. I do not even remember dressing for the fight.

My opponent, fearful that I had been killed, called upon me while I was still unconscious. A kindly note scrawled with pencil begged my forgiveness.

Some minutes after I opened my eyes I vaguely grasped the situation. The note began, "You were knocked out last night—"

Still shaky, I went to the lobby, and from there to the street.

Years of struggle followed before Tully established himself as a successful writer with the publication of his first book in 1922. But by 1935, Tully's last two books had tanked, and, in the view of many, Tully had peaked as a writer. Beset by personal problems and jaded by the tinniness of Hollywood, Tully was at a crossroads when he met Langston Hughes, a longtime admirer of Tully's work, at a Beverly Hills party. The two writers hit it off, and Tully invited Hughes to come by some time for lunch.

When Hughes called a couple days later, he asked if he might bring Harry Armstrong, a former boxer turned trainer who wanted to write. Tully quickly consented and a date was set. Hughes and Armstrong planned on taking the interurban from downtown Los Angeles to Tully's home, an hour and a half ride. Harry's protege, Henry Jackson, who had even taken his mentor's name and boxed as Henry Armstrong, was free that morning and offered to drive the men and wait in the car. When they arrived, Hughes mentioned that the young boxer was waiting outside in the car and Tully immediately went out to invite Henry to join them.

Like Langston Hughes and Jim Tully, so too does it seem that Henry Armstrong and Tully were destined to meet. In his autobiography, *Gloves, Glory and God,* Armstrong remembered laying awake one night in St. Louis when he felt the irresistible pull of California. It was the heart of the Depression, and neither Henry nor his trainer and running buddy, Harry, had anything like train fare to California. Writing in the third-person, Armstrong recalled,

> Well, if there wasn't money for the trip, maybe it could be made without money. He had read somewhere of an author named Jim Tully, who had been a fighter and a hobo. If Tully could make it all over the country as a hobo, surely Henry could get to California that way.

They caught a west-bound freight train in Carondelet, Missouri, and a few years later washed up at Tully's Toluca Lake door. Tully liked Armstrong immediately. "When he entered the room," Tully wrote, "I knew at once there was a man in the house." Armstrong was mostly silent but listened intently as his trainer and Hughes described how tough it was for a boxer to make a living. Tully could only nod in recognition. Armstrong had lost fixed matches with the Mexican fighter, Baby Arizmendi, that he'd clearly won and was as broke in Los Angeles as he had been in St. Louis. "You might see a way out, Jim," Hughes said. "Henry's beaten him twice and lost two decisions—he's innocent and honest, and it isn't right." To make matters worse, Wirt Ross, who bought Armstrong's contract when the boxer was a minor, had scheduled him to again fight Arizmendi. Moved by the hobo-turned-boxer's plight, one he knew firsthand, Tully impulsively raised the possibility of buying Armstrong's contract from Ross. Armstrong was very enthusiastic, leaving Tully to mull it over. Watching his guests leave, Tully regretted not hearing more from the young boxer. "My God," he later commented, "a great man has been here. Armstrong was the wisest of us all. He saved his breath for the pork chops."

The prospect of a return to boxing, albeit outside the ropes, was tempting.

> For days the idea burned in my head. I would again enter the wild world of the bruiser. The thought made the bubbles burst in my blood. It would be a return to the care-free days I'd loved. I had fought hard for freedom and found it another jail.

It is a measure of how miserable Tully had become that he considered boxing as way out of writing, rather than the reverse. In the end, he came to the conclusion he'd reached more than two decades before and chose writing over boxing. Tully instead promised to speak to Al Jolson, who had both the interest and means to promote a young boxer. Tully's decision not to buy Armstrong's contract seems not to have hurt Armstrong in the least. Armstrong fought another ten years and for a few months in late 1938 simultaneously held the World's Featherweight, Welterweight, and Lightweight Championships. Armstrong was elected to the Boxing Hall of Fame in 1954.

Boxing was one thing; *writing* about boxing was another. In his 1934 *Esquire* essay "The Manly Art," Tully wrote, "The great book of the prize ring is yet to be written. The man who will write it will be one who has been smeared with its blood." While litterateurs as diverse as George Bernard Shaw and Ernest Hemingway had tried, none had boxed and could hope to really convey what it was like inside the ropes. Two years later, tired of waiting for an honest novel of the ring, Tully decided to write it himself.

By early September he had a first draft and had built up a head of steam in the writing of a novel about a young boxer named Shane Rory. He could feel it in his bones, the boxing novel was going to be good, *very* good. This one would restore his good name and get him the respect that he felt was his due. The past year had been one of survival, but now there was hope and he could finally feel his long depression beginning to lift. Two weeks later he was knocked off the tracks.

Tully's son, Alton, had been arrested for assaulting a 16-year-old girl. It was not the first such incident and the news made headlines across the country. Concerned friends tried to lift Tully's spirits, and it is worth noting that another former drifter-turned-boxer, Jack Dempsey, phoned with the offer of $10,000 to help with legal expenses. Tully was devastated, and work on the boxing novel came to a halt. Instead, he returned to the question he'd faced most of his adult life: What to do about Alton? In the past, he'd come to the boy's defense, but this time, against all paternal instinct and the advice of Alton's attorneys, he insisted Alton plead guilty. This Alton did and was sentenced to San Quentin for one to fifty years.

Tully looked to crawl from the wreckage with a new book. He sounded out Maxwell Perkins, who had become renowned as the editor of Fitzgerald, Hemingway, and Thomas Wolfe, on a boxing book but was torn between the novel about Shane Rory or a history of the ring. He felt it necessary to convince the legendary editor that he was not a has-been. "I've played in bad luck the past few years, and have done considerable movie work, but I'm by no means out of the running as a writer."

Tully was far from a has-been, but his year-end royalty statement punctuated a bad year. *Ladies in the Parlor,* his previous book, had earned him just $200 in the past six months of 1935. Perkins declined a boxing history but asked to see the novel. Tully returned to the Shane Rory manuscript, now titled *The Bruiser,* he'd been working on before the tribulations of autumn. Perkins was not enthusiastic about the draft he received of *The Bruiser,* and, for the time being, the two went their separate ways.

With a solid draft of *The Bruiser* in hand, Tully began shopping the book around. Having immersed himself in boxing, he flew to New York in April to work with Jack Dempsey on a play based on the legendary champion's life. Waiting for him on his return was a letter with the happy news that his 1934 federal tax return was going to be audited.

Tully first sent *The Bruiser* to Boni, the publisher of two of his earlier novels, who wanted the manuscript so badly that he signed away the film rights. By late June, Tully had misgivings about signing with Boni and his request to be released from his contract was granted. Frustrated with what he saw as Jim's fussiness over publishers, Tully's agent, Sydney Sanders, quit, leaving Jim free to strike his own deal for *The Bruiser.*

Hoping that the *The Bruiser* would make a bigger splash with Simon & Schuster, who had rejected *Ladies in the Parlor,* Tully mailed the manuscript in July to editor and friend H. L. Mencken, who hand-delivered it to Max Schuster. With Tully now years away from having anything like a successful book, the rejection a few weeks later from Simon & Schuster rattled his confidence. He wrote Mencken, "I am not hurt much, as I have such contempt for the novel, that I know I'm not much good at the writing of one."

In the end he returned to his old publisher, Greenberg, mailing a draft of *The Bruiser* in late July and signed a contract shortly after. However, Greenberg's insistence that *The Bruiser* have a happy ending gave Tully pause. Greenberg was not alone in finding problems with the book's conclusion. Mencken found the ending "abrupt."

Whatever the problems with the book's conclusion, Tully was determined that the boxing scenes would be the best ever written. Many writers had written about boxing but none had Tully's experience inside the ropes. Tully even recruited his pal, former heavyweight contender Frank Moran, to shadowbox the final fight and then had Dempsey read the manuscript.

Greenberg got right to work soliciting blurbs from Gene Fowler, Walter Winchell, Mencken, and Frank Scully. He also contacted George Bellows's estate for permission to use his masterpiece, *Stag at Sharkey's,* for the dust jacket. The executor declined but wrote Greenberg, "If I could say yes to anyone it would be you for Mr. Tully's novel."

By early August, Tully had rewritten the conclusion. As one reporter described it,

It was to end with the girl sending the discouraged fighter back to the ring with lusty admonitions about the old gutseroo and courage and try-try-again and I'll-be-waiting. So the guy goes back to the ring and finally he becomes champ but in the process he gets lobbed around until he's slug-nutty. Punch drunk. So he goes back to the Girl and marries her and she's got a slap-happy, drooling champ on her hands for the rest of her life.

This was not the happy ending Greenberg wanted, and, with yet another ending, Tully delivered the completed manuscript that September. *The Bruiser* was set for release later in the fall. Mencken wrote, "If I were still editor of *The American Mercury,* your description of that prize fight would already be in type." Returning to the bout in another letter, he concluded, "it is one of the best things anybody has ever done." Greenberg was equally optimistic and asked for a proposal for Tully's next book. A month later, Greenberg's mood darkened. He complained that advanced sales for *The Bruiser* were poor, citing resistance from booksellers and women to boxing novels. Tully, never known for patience with his publishers, could hardly be blamed for being irritated. Greenberg was well aware that he was publishing a boxing novel and pronouncing a book a failure before a single review appeared was premature at best.

With his mood still soured by Greenberg's dire forecast about *The Bruiser,* Tully's career hit bottom when a letter from Bennett Cerf, the publisher of The Modern Library, landed on his desk with a thud. Cerf declined to reprint any of Tully's earlier books, noting that "I have done some quiet checking up on the sale of these books in the last few years, however, and am sorry to say that I find the demand, in New York at least, is practically nil." All hope rested with *The Bruiser.*

Novelists who choose sports as a central theme face a common pitfall. If, at the novel's conclusion, the protagonist proves the odds surmountable and knocks out his opponent or hits a home run with two outs in the ninth, most readers will leave thinking they've just finished a boilerplate boy's book. If the hero lands on the canvas or strikes out at the book's conclusion, readers will understandably feel let down. The best sports novels and films wisely avoid this trap, from the baseball books *Blue Ruin* by Brendan Boyd and *Shoeless Shoe* by W. P. Kinsella to such films as John Sayles's *Eight Men Out* and Martin Scorsese's *Raging Bull*. Each succeeds by not aligning its story with a particular contest.

The Bruiser follows Shane Rory from his days as a road kid, through his unsteady ascent up the boxing ranks, and culminates in his title fight for the heavyweight championship. With the book so structured, Tully's problems with the ending were inevitable. His solution was to have Shane Rory win the title fight and hand over the crown to a black boxer and fellow road kid whose route to the top would have otherwise been blocked by a color line. It was a happy ending to be sure but with a twist. If the conclusion of *The Bruiser* seems a bit pat, the thirty-one chapters which precede it are not. Shane Rory, like Jim Tully was an accidental fighter. He tried boxing, won his fight, and, "The course of his life changed. He was a combination road kid and wandering fighter."

The description of road kid and fighter could only have been written by one who knew both road and ring intimately. The action inside the ropes bristles with jabs, hooks, crosses, and uppercuts. And when Tully has a veteran boxer tell Shane, "I like you, that's all—you take it and lash it out—and you don't whimper," he is repeating almost word for word Jim's own code, stated to Langston Hughes months earlier. While Tully paints Shane in heroic colors, *The Bruiser* avoids sentimentality. It takes an unflinching look at all the types who encrust boxing, including broken-down punch-drunks, gamblers, cheats, hangers-on, promoters, reporters, and fans screaming for blood.

Recalling Jim's experiences, Shane's life is transformed by books, or, in Shane's case, one book in particular: Helen Keller's *Story of My Life*. Reading the book in one sitting, Shane closes Keller's memoir and realizes that despite Keller's blindness and deafness, "She's seen more than I have." Shane "had never been aware of bees and flowers. The blind girl had. The world was a place he had never known." It is one of Tully's favorite themes: a damaged life transformed by a book.

Reviews of *The Bruiser* were the best Tully had received in years and among the best he'd ever had. *New York Times* critic E. C. Beckwith acknowledged the novel followed the standard formula for boxing books, but recognized that Tully had "manipulated them with so skillful an artistry that the resultant work acquires a freshness and vitality which one had long ago thought extinct in pugilistic fiction." There is a "touch of heart interest," Beckwith continued,

> But it is in discourses expressed through his characters on ring science, in his descriptions of fistic events, in his first-hand knowledge of the game in every department, that Mr. Tully comes very close to writing, in *The Bruiser,* the best novel of its type this reviewer has read in late years.

David Tilden, critic at *Books,* noted that *The Bruiser* was not "literary in any sense of the word, but the story is swiftly moving and, with just enough of disorder and emotion to make it a thoroughly human document."

Frank Scully picked up on Tully's description of a punch-drunk boxer in his review of the *The Bruiser*. The subject had received scant attention before *The Bruiser* and Scully was taken with Tully's accurate portrayal. Tully's punch-drunk reminded Scully of Ad Wolgast, "a once prominent bruiser who ended his ring career throwing punches at shuffling phantoms in the cell of an insane asylum."

Wolgast was indeed the basis for Tully's punch-drunk boxer. Jim had kept tabs on his former sparring partner, who had been sent to the Camarillo State Hospital in 1927 and where he remained for the rest of his life. In addition to basing *The Bruiser*'s Adam Walsh on Wolgast, Tully used Joe Gans as the basis for Joe Crane, Jack Tierney for Chicago Jed Williams, and Battling Schultz for Battling Ryan.

Jim was buoyed by the good reviews, writing Nathan, "The novel, 'Bruiser' is starting well—400 copies sold yesterday. . . . It's the starting of my second wind." And to Mencken, Tully could crow that *The Bruiser* was proving to be his best book "critically and financially" since 1929.

Praise for *The Bruiser* arrived from other quarters as well. Former heavyweight champion Gene Tunney, who had defeated Jack Dempsey twice, wrote to thank Jim for his inscribed copy, "It has great dramatic quality and from the pugilistic point of view is technically perfect." Damon Runyon called it the greatest story of the ring ever told. W. C. Fields thanked Jim for his copy, adding in typically Fieldsian fashion, "Not a spoonful of the vile stuff has passed underneath my ruby nose these five months." Nella Braddy, biographer of Anne Sullivan Macy, wrote on behalf of Helen

Keller to say that "*The Bruiser* reached Miss Helen Keller's home in the midst of the greatest sorrow of her life—the death on Oct. 20 of the great Irishwoman, Anne Sullivan Macy, who had been her teacher and constant companion for forty-nine years." Braddy told Miss Keller about the book on the train returning from the funeral. "She was very much touched to know that you had thought of using her in the way you did and asked me to thank you." Not all notices were so sublime. Alton wrote his stepmother from San Quentin,

> *The Bruiser* is going over with a bang here—everyone is asking to read it, some getting half sore when I let someone else read it before them. The average reader gets to the Cyclone fight on the 1st night before the lights go out—and comes to me the next marveling and talking of it, I think 'Wait until you reach the Sully fight' sure enough they come out raving about it with a half dozen friends in tow asking to get on the line for it.... The old fighters rave about it more than the rest—all agree that dad is the master of his subject.

In a lifetime of impossible odds, *The Bruiser* marked the triumphant comeback of an American writer who had learned early in life one important lesson: Never stop punching.

THE BRUISER

I

It was raining fiercely. The clouds roared with thunder. Water fell in long silver slivers. There was no escape from the driving water. Under the projecting roof of the section house, Shane Rory stood and gazed at the water splashing on the rails. His clothes were wet and wind-whipped.

He was about eighteen, and had not reached full growth. In spite of the rain, his hair still curled at the edge of his cap. A large blue scarf was tied about his neck. His coat collar was turned up. His hands were deep in his pockets. His jaws were set, his forehead wrinkled as he tried to penetrate through the rain-splashed air.

Engines shrieked about the railroad yards, their headlights burnishing the falling water.

He heard a voice coming near,

> "It tain't no use to grumble
> an' complain—
> It's jes' as cheap an' easy
> to rejoice—
> When God sohts out de weatheh
> an' sends rain;
> Den rain's mah choice—"

A young Negro tramp joined him. Coffee-colored, good-looking, and about Shane's age, he removed a cap that was plastered to his head with water.

The light from an engine slanted across him, as he said, "Lordy golly—what a night!"

"Wet, huh," smiled Shane.

"Wet ain't de name," he said, ringing the water from his cap, "I think some pipes is busted up theah." His teeth showed white and even as he laughed. "It purty neah washed de train off de track comin' in heah," he said as the wind swerved and threw the rain in their faces. "Hold on theah, Mister God, quit slappin' us wit' dat wateh—we's all had a bath." The young Negro looked upward and laughed again. There was a smile in Shane's eyes.

"I'd give mah home in Heaben for a drink right now —and believe you me, I'd never take it back neitheh."

He wore a ragged, red sweater and a wide-checked coat much too large for him.

"I wondeh what all de pooh people's doin' tonight— heah we is nice an' wahm afteh a big dinneh—an' a lot of pooh folks is outen de rain."

A switchman signaled an engine about fifty feet away.

Shane grabbed the Negro's arm. "Come with me," he said.

The water ran in rivulets from the switchman's rubber raincoat.

"How far is it to the nearest saloon?" Shane asked the man.

He lifted the lantern in Shane's face. "It's about three

hundred yards across the tracks," he said, pointing.

"Thanks—let's go." Shane pulled the Negro's arm.

A few minutes later their shoes squished with water across the dry floor of the empty saloon.

The bartender's eyes narrowed at Shane's companion.

"We don't serve Niggers in here," he said.

"But, Mister," Shane said, "I never thought of that —he's been in the hospital, sick—and he's been outen the rain. There's nobody here—won't you?"

"Well, I'll sell it to you, and you give it to him—let's see the color of your money."

The bartender took the dollar, filled two glasses to the brim, and rang up twenty cents. When he turned from the register, the glasses were empty.

"Fill 'em up," Shane ordered.

The bartender's eyes widened.

"How old are you kids?"

"Twenty-one—what's the difference?" Shane said.

"This Nigger kid's not over seventeen."

"Sure he is," said Shane— "Do you want to wire back to his home and find out?"

"Where, Africa—?" The bartender laughed, and filled the glasses.

Shane pushed a half dollar toward the Negro. "We might get split up," he said,—"keep this."

"I shuah will—thank you."

The liquor tingling, they turned from the bar.

"Have one on me," said the bartender. "I wouldn't want to see even a railroad dick out on a night like this." He looked sharply at Shane. "You're a nice lookin' kid—how long you been a bum?"

"Ever since I can remember," was the answer.

"And you?" He turned to the Negro.

"Afore that."

He placed two full glasses in front of Shane, who handed one to his dark companion.

The switchman who had directed them to the saloon entered. "All the crazy people ain't in the bug-house," he said to the bartender, looking in Shane's direction.

The bartender drained a glass and said, "Here's good luck, 'boes."

"Is it still raining?" Shane asked the switchman.

"Nope—it's about cleared up—which way are you fellows headed?"

"West," was Shane's answer.

"Well, there's a fast freight through in an hour. She's headed West, and she slows up over the trestle." Again he pointed.

Shane bought a half pint of liquor.

As they left the saloon, the bartender again said, "Good luck."

They had not gone far when the rain began again. With heads down, they hurried onward. The thunder roared. The rain splashed.

"This'll make us grow," laughed Shane.

"It'll wash me so white my ma won't know me." Again came the Negro boy's musical laugh. "It's too wet foh ducks eben."

He turned to Shane, "Gimme a drink o' dat liquor?"

"You can have it. I don't want any more."

"Thanks." The dark boy lifted the bottle.

The rain hit the bottom and rolled with the liquor into his mouth.

"May's well get wet inside as out," he said. He looked at the half empty bottle.

As if he had dropped from the clouds with the rain, another young fellow joined them.

The yellow headlight from a switch-engine revealed him as dark, alert, almost handsome, and not over twenty-five.

"Which way, 'boes?" he asked.

"Either way," returned Shane, "mostly West."

"Can I string along?" Without waiting for an answer, he saw the bottle in the Negro vagabond's hand and said, "What's you got there?"

"Puhfume," laughed the Negro, "We's scentin' up the air."

The light from the engine moved closer.

Both white boys looked at the powerful young Negro.

"I'se goin' somewheah's to sleep," he said, "Torpedo Jones am all tiahed out."

"What you tired out about?" asked the young fellow who had recently joined them.

"I wuz in a battle royal fouh nights ago—I done had to lick seben otheh Niggahs for five dollahs—an' I ain't got rested yit—I ain't." He shuffled a few feet with an ominous grace. "I'se goin' to be a prize-fighteh—it's easier'n gittin' caught'n de rain an' nowheah's to sleep." He chuckled deep in his throat. "Boy—did dem Niggahs trow dem punches—dey kep' a whizzin' by like bullets wit' grease on 'em—dey was moah Niggahs in dat ring den dey is in jail—ebery time I stahts to poke, some Niggah'd wham me on de jaw—an' dat las' Niggah befoah ah knock 'im dayd—he buhns one acrost ma ches' like a red hot pokah—but dat was de las'. I hits 'im so hahd I jes' blas' his brains right outta de top o' his head—if dem ropes haden been deah—he'd be a rollin' yit." He looked at his brown fist— "Yes suh—boy—when I hits 'em dey stays hit—when dat battle royal was ober dem Niggahs wuz layin' aroun' dat ring like dey'd been shot—"

The rain pelting his wide shoulders, he sauntered, cat-like, away.

"I'll bet he can fight," volunteered Shane.

"What'd he call himself?" asked his companion.

"Torpedo Jones."

The two white boys drifted together westward for about a week before arriving in a town of ten thousand people.

"Let's look the place over and meet at the depot in a couple of hours," Shane's companion suggested.

"Okeh," returned Shane.

He waited for the young fellow at the depot.

"Well, how did you make out?" he asked.

"Fine. I've got a job," he said, "The priest gave me ten dollars to put gilt on his altar. It'll take me a couple of days, and you can help me. He's giving me twenty dollars altogether for the job. I told him I was an interior decorator." He showed a ten dollar bill. "Let's get some grub first—then I'll buy the stuff and we'll go to work."

An hour later they reported to the priest. He took them into the church and explained what he wanted done; then left.

No sound could be heard inside. Even their footsteps were indistinct around the heavy carpeted altar. The Lamp of the Sanctuary burned low, and in late afternoon threw faint shadows over them.

At the finish of their work, Shane's companion took him by the arm. Together they walked around the church, stopping at each painting that depicted Christ on His journey through life and death to the final resurrection.

At the last picture, Shane's comrade, solemn until now, said quickly, "He didn't have so much luck either."

The priest entered, going slowly to the altar. The boys moved toward him.

Standing beneath the Lamp of the Sanctuary, he rubbed his hands together, and with a rapt expression, said, "I am pleased indeed. You have made it shine like the glory of God."

He was a roly-poly man, who waddled slightly as he walked. He had two heavy chins, a florid complexion, and wore heavy glasses over his eyes.

After he had paid the rest of the money, he shook hands with each boy, saying, "Return to your homes, children—you are both too bright to lead such lives."

They had not gone far, when Shane's companion said, "I hope he don't get next before we get out of town."

"Next to what?" Shane asked.

"It was radiator gilt I put on the altar. It'll turn green in wet weather." He looked up at the clouding sky.

"That's a shame," Shane said, "he trusted you."

"Well, real gilt would of cost ten dollars. I got enough radiator gilt for three."

"Well, let me go back and tell him—it'll only make it hard on someone else that wants a favor from him." Shane started back.

The young fellow held his arm and said, "It's done now. If you tell him we may both get pinched."

Clouds covered the moon. The rain could be seen coming over the mountains. It continued steadily for more than an hour.

Shane and his companion stood in front of a well-lit store.

Two policemen approached them.

Shane's companion said hurriedly, "Let's go," and ran swiftly away.

Shane stood still.

The older policeman held him. The younger one chased his companion.

They were taken to the jail.

"Why did you run?" Shane asked his companion, after they were booked on suspicion, and placed in a cell.

Ill at ease, he answered, "I thought the priest squealed."

They were brought before the Chief of Police, and questioned next morning. When finished with Shane, he said, "We'll hold you a while for further investigation."

His companion stepped forward. The Chief looked at him and grunted, "Ever see that?" He showed the youth his portrait.

The youth's face blanched.

He had escaped from an Eastern penitentiary while serving a term for burglary.

"Take them away," commanded the Chief.

They were put in separate cells.

Shane heard his companion sobbing.

When they were turned loose in the yard for exercise, Shane said, "I wish I could do something."

"I wish you could too," he said, "but it's too late now." He became more hopeful, "But five years ain't so long."

The priest held services in the jail on Sunday.

The boys hung their heads as he came toward them.

He greeted them kindly, with a sad expression in his eyes.

"Do not be afraid," he said, "I will say nothing." He looked at Shane's companion, "You have trouble enough." The priest's lips trembled. He concealed with an effort the agony in his heart.

Shane was sent for the next morning. The priest was in the office of the Chief of Police.

"We're turning you loose," said the Chief. "Father Downey here has given you a job."

"Yes," said the priest, "I would like to have you gild my altar. It has turned green."

"All right, Father, I'll be glad to," said Shane.

When Shane had finished, the priest paid for his room and meals and gave him ten dollars.

"Come with me to the jail," he said. "The poor boy is going East tonight."

Arriving there, the priest put an arm about the youth, and said, "Too bad."

Shane and the priest stood for some moments upon the depot platform after the train had gone.

When it had faded from sight, the priest said slowly, "May he find mercy in the bosom of Christ, our Lord."

The Chief of Police approached. "You know in our 'Smoker' tomorrow night, Father, the boy in the first preliminary's sick."

Shane spoke up. "Let me take his place. I can fight."

The Chief looked surprised.

"What's your name, Jim Corbett?"

"No, Terry McGovern."

The priest's eyes twinkled. "I wonder if you're lyin'."

The stern policeman smiled.

"You look like you might be able to go some."

"He does indeed." The priest's eyes went over Shane. "You're a whelp of a boy."

"Well, I won't let you down, Father."

"Can you really box?" asked the Chief.

"Quite a bit," answered Shane.

The engine that took his companion to the penitentiary whistled far away.

"Dear, dear," said the priest, "it's such a sad world."

II

Shane experienced none of the stage fright common to those who first enter the ring. The enclosure was so heavy with smoke that faces in the audience were indistinct.

"Just remember," his second, a withered old fighter volunteered, "the other fellow's scared as you."

"He's not much scared if he ain't," Shane grinned.

He sat in the ring, in borrowed canvas shoes too large for him, and tights that hung loosely about his loins. A pair of worn leather cracked boxing gloves were fastened upon his hands.

He could hear the priest saying, "Good luck, my boy."

The second grinned as he patted Shane's gloves, "Yeah, Kid—say one 'Our Father' and one 'Hail Mary' that you knock his block off quick."

"I don't need to pray for that—you watch."

"You're a cocky little devil—but that's what it takes."

The gong rang.

He went toward his opponent with hands in hitting position.

Instinctively, his first time in the ring, he did not step to the left, or lead with one hand and chop with the other, but glided gracefully in and out of striking distance.

In less than a minute, his rival, a formidable looking Mexican boy, was on the floor.

Shane was given twenty-five dollars.

He was amazed at the amount. He would work two weeks for that much. And he had earned it in a couple of minutes.

The course of his life changed. He was a combination of road kid and wandering fighter.

The boy he had whipped was from Phoenix. Waiting until the newspaper came out next morning, he bought several copies and went to that city, and located the leading newspaper. The Mexican was known as a promising fighter in his home town. Within a few days he was again matched with the boy he had knocked out.

The matchmaker gave him an advance of fifty dollars. It was a good match for him. Thousands of Mexicans would come to see a fellow-countryman.

Shane made his headquarters at a small gymnasium on Centre Street.

The newspapers printed stories of his exploits in other cities. Soon he was a celebrity. He bought a new sweater and other articles of clothing to go with his changed position in life.

Training at the same gymnasium was a one-time well known fighter named Spider Smith. Shane absorbed his mannerisms, and boxed with him daily. After each encounter, he realized how much stronger he was than Smith, who was a middleweight. Shane was lighter.

On Sunday, an admission of twenty-five cents was

charged to see him box with Smith. This helped to defray the small expenses of training.

Each morning he would run for five miles. He learned to know each sign along the road. He would often wave at people as they watched him.

He won again in sensational manner. His opponent went down three times in the fourth.

He was next matched with a young miner from Bisbee. After training two weeks, the miner was taken ill. The fight was declared off. His purse against the Mexican had been two hundred and thirty dollars. With what remained, he left for El Paso, where Smith had said "the game was good."

Taking Smith with him, they loitered about the Texas city and its Mexican environs for several weeks.

In Juarez, he met a boxing promoter from Mexico City. Smith, acting as manager, explained Shane's defeat of the Mexican boy in Phoenix.

The promoter watched Shane "work out" in a gymnasium the next afternoon. Impressed, he took him to Mexico City. Smith went along as manager and trainer.

Shane's match was the third on an "all star card." The high altitude of Mexico City affected him. Unable to breathe properly, he lost in the sixth round.

He parted with Smith the next day. "I'm headin' for Vera Cruz," said Smith, "then on to Buenos Aires —they throw gloves too fast for me in the States—"

Smith looked about the ancient red railroad station where Shane waited for his train to be called. "Now don't take this lickin' to heart, kid," he said, "No one'll ever know you've been down here by the time you're a top notcher—you can change your name a little later—or keep this outta your record—if you ever go far places it's all right with me—I'm never comin' back to the States anyhow—I've had enough."

"How long you been fightin'?" asked Shane.

"Too long—all my life—but only in the ring twenty-one years—that's older'n you are, kid. I've made a barrel of dough in my time—had dames in silks and satins, and smooth as new gloves. They're all gone now—and I'm sneakin' out of the picture with nothin' to do but remember—it comes to all of us; so what-inhell's the difference—none of it's worth a damn."

The road had taught Shane observation. Smith's eyes were sharp. His eagle-face had not been made shapeless by the many gloves that had battered against it.

The train for El Paso was called. Shane held his worn handbag, and said, "So long, Old Timer, it was good knowin' you."

"Same here, Kid, I'll be thinkin' about you—you'll get somewhere—you've got a lot—you can take that Kid Pueblo if you ever get him off a mountain—and—if anyone·ever talks to you about Spider Smith just don't say a word. I'm just oozin' out of the picture like I oozed into it. When a guy who ain't a fighter brags about how good a man he used to be, nobody cares much—it's like kids braggin'."

"You said something, Spider, about me keepin' this outta my record—I won't if this Pueblo's good enough to get credit. Maybe that's all he'll have to brag about by the time I'm champion. He can stroll around this town and the little brown-eyed dolls can say, 'There goes Pueblo. He stopped Shane Rory' or whatever they say in Mexican—"

"He didn't stop you, Kid—you just couldn't breathe."

"But I'll wipe it out if I ever get him in the States."

The train started to move at last.

"So long—"

"So long—"

After a few hours on the train, his fight with Kid Pueblo became clearer. With the ego of the great, born fighter, he did not realize that Pueblo had too much experience for him, and might have at least won the decision anywhere. "He never hurt me," Shane thought.

Smith had sent a telegram to the sporting editor of an El Paso paper, explaining the defeat. He would save the paper. He might get Pueblo in Phoenix. He had to do something soon.

His mind rested on Spider Smith.

He had been reading about him for years. "One of the cleverest men in the world—if he could only hit." He wondered why some men could hit, and others couldn't. Pueblo was a hard hitter. "He'll never get to the top—he telegraphs his punches. . . . Just how does a fellow get to the top?" he had asked Spider Smith.

"He's got to have everything—and a lot of luck," Smith had replied.

Smith remained long in the boy's thoughts.

Next morning, another American boarded the train.

He wore a blue suit, faded yellow from the sun, and a wide gray felt hat with a leather strap around it.

After a day's silence, Shane was glad to talk.

"Which way, Mister?"

"Indiana." The man's blue eyes, sun-faded like his suit, looked kindly at the young fighter. "And you?"

"El Paso," Shane answered.

"Been down here long?"

"Nope—a few weeks—had a fight down here—the climate got me—I'm goin' back."

"Who'd you fight?"

"Kid Pueblo."

"He's a good man."

"Yeah, I know," returned Shane.

The stranger was a mining engineer. His wife had left Mexico eight weeks before. Both thought she would have better care in Indiana. She was now dead in childbirth. The wire came the night before. They lived in a small cottage near the mine for two years. He had locked the door on it forever. He would return to Mexico though. "It gets you after a time—the stars and the sky and the night."

Shane wanted to ask a question. Finally he said, "And the little baby?"

"It's alive," the father raised his eyes, "I traded one for the other," his voice choked, "but that's the way it goes."

Shane had bought a few curios. Taking a little stone image from his bag, he said, "Give this to the baby, won't you?"

"Surely," the man's eyes rested on Shane—"thanks, that's kind of you."

"Well, you know, I just bought 'em. I ain't got anybody."

"That's too bad—we all ought to have something."

"Yes, I guess so," Shane returned vaguely.

They parted at El Paso.

"I'm flying from here," said the mining engineer.

"Good luck," said Shane. "I'm goin' on to Phoenix."

He bought a paper that explained his loss to Kid Pueblo.

"You're a smart kid—you don't need no manager," the promoter at Phoenix said, "but I can't get Kid Pueblo here—too much money. Freddy Garcia beat a pretty good boy last week. I can steam you two up again—winner to meet Kid Pueblo—that'll go good."

Again he defeated Garcia.

He loitered about Phoenix for several days. The hot season was approaching. There would soon be no more matches until cooler weather.

The promoter said, "I can get you a few hundred over in Prescott against Garcia."

"I can't go on lickin' him forever," said Shane.

"You'll not lick him this time—let him get a draw— that'll build him up for Phoenix again—his manager tells me he'll give you half his purse—for ten rounds."

"No, I don't want to do that. I'd forget in there anyhow when the goin' got rough—and then I'd be a double-crosser."

"Well, leave it to me. I'll make the match—go in and fight."

"All right."

Though Shane tried all the way, Garcia not only stayed the limit, but earned a draw.

Shane could not understand.

When Garcia's manager wanted to give him half the purse, Shane would not accept. "He fought hard for it—let him have it."

"You're a mighty good sport," said the manager.

"Not so good," returned Shane, who had learned one of the mysteries of the ring—that on an "off night" a champion might lose to a dub.

"If you ever hit Omaha," said the manager, "go to Buck Logan, sports editor on the *Post*—he's good people—I'll write him about you."

The urge of the road returned. He drifted about the country for several weeks, with money sewed in different parts of his clothing.

His money about all gone, he arrived in Wichita, where a fight between two high-ranking lightweights of the Middle West was to be held on the last day of the convention of independent oil dealers.

He applied to Jack Gill, one of the contestants, for a job as sparring partner. The training camp was pitched along the Arkansas River.

"Think you can take 'em?" Gill's manager asked Shane.

"Yes, I think so."

"Well, get in there with Gill this afternoon—if you give him a good workout, I'll give you a job—five bucks a day and your board. It's ten days to the fight—that'll get you fifty iron men."

The camp was crowded when he squared off with Gill. At once Gill began to "give him the works." After a rapid exchange, it was Gill who "broke ground." At the end of the four rounds, he patted Shane on the shoulder, "You'll do, Kid."

Now a member of the camp, he did road work each morning with Gill who learned to like him.

Gill was a steel worker from a town in Illinois. Like Shane, he became a fighter by accident.

When one of the pugilists, billed for the semi-wind-up, hurt his hand, Gill suggested that Shane take his place. The purse was three hundred dollars, sixty percent to the winner.

"You'll have to give away about ten pounds," explained Gill, "but you can't do any worse than lose the decision. Maley throws a lot of punches but can't hit hard enough to break an Easter egg. He's rough—but don't let that worry you—I beat him two years ago. Keep in on him—never stop punchin'—he's got a six round heart—after that he wilts. He got a draw with Jerry Wayne and he's been travelin' on that ever since."

Shane always remembered the ten days with Jack Gill. A murderous puncher, he was cruel in workouts, but always fair. He did not play to the gallery. Neither did he ask his sparring partners to pull their punches. "If they're men enough to whip me, I've got no business among the top notchers."

His manager knew little of the fight game. A foreman in a steel mill, Jack Gill had carried him along. Gill had worked in the mill until money was assured in the ring.

Thirty thousand people were at the fight.

"We've raised your six rounder to ten—just to give the folks a show," the promoter explained to Shane— "and we've anted the purse up to five hundred. Is that okeh?"

"You bet. Suppose I knock him out?"

"You can get three to one that says you can't."

"Well—even if I lose the duke I got forty percent of five hundred, ain't I?"

"Why yes."

"Will you bet a hundred of that dough that I knock him out?"

Jack Gill spoke up— "Cut me in on another hundred of that—and another century that if there's a knockout Rory here'll land it. Phone it to the papers how I stand."

"Thanks, Jack—you're swell."

Shane's arm went round his employer.

On the night of the fight, Gill said, "Now listen, Kid—throw punches till you die—you got a hundred bucks on yourself—three to one—suppose you click— and sixty percent of five hundred—now don't spar a second. Throw punches—keep in—the minute he backs up, push right in again—I tell you he's got a six round heart—he can't hurt you if I couldn't."

The western sky was still red when the first preliminary went on.

Shane used Gill's dressing-room.

"Now make it snappy, Kid. I'll wait here till you come back. I'll want you swingin' that towel over me."

Rory went down the aisle.

"It's one of those things," Gill said to his manager. "That kid's got a bulldog's heart—and he's fast as a greyhound—watch."

Other sparring mates from Gill's camp attended Shane. Maley was contemptuous.

"Gunner Maley," he bowed to the introduction, "meets Shane Rory—ten rounds—moved up from six for your benefit. Rory, lest we forget, is a protégé of Jack Gill's—five thousand dollars is wagered on the result of this fight. Three to one—if there's a knockout, Rory will land it." The announcer clapped his hands. The referee stepped to the centre of the ring.

Maley, with bull neck, and powerful shoulders, the gloves already on his hands, stepped from his corner.

A hush came over the gathering.

Rory came to meet him.

Lithe, his body sun-burned about the shoulders and neck, his ribs wash-board indented, a few freckles across his nose, his lips tight set, his hair a mass of packed curls, he slapped one glove against another while the referee gave instructions.

The referee stopped.

"Are you through?" Maley asked.

"Yes."

"No fouls now—everything goes—this is a fight."

"Yes," snapped Rory— "This is a fight."

Scowling, Maley dashed to his corner. The gong rang.

Maley rushed. His blows failed to bring Rory from his shell. A few cracked against the top of Shane's head hard enough to drive it between his shoulders.

Rory came forward, ignoring Maley's head. He stamped with his left foot, feinted with right and left hand, drew back, then planted his right foot deep in the canvas.

Maley charged.

An ox would have fallen under the battering. So did Maley. So swift and terrible were the blows that Maley caught them on the way down.

The audience groaned from the sudden finish.

"I knew it, by God, I knew it," Jack Gill said— "throw some clothes on him—rub him off later—I'll stall in the ring till he comes."

Before final instructions were given, Shane crawled through the ropes. Roars of applause followed.

"Bow, Kid, bow"—Gill snapped.

Shane acknowledged the applause.

Gill, not so fortunate as Shane, received a close decision over his opponent.

"You were up against a better man than me," Shane consoled.

"Not at all, Kid—it's the game—a woman's liable to lick you the night you think you can whip an army. You were *right* tonight—you could of licked Stanley Ketchell—that's all—but I will say—that louse I fought's nobody's stumble-bum."

"I'll say he's not," said Shane, "He don't stumble even when you hit him."

"If he does," smiled Gill, "it's back for more. I

thought my hands were bone dust, I hit him so hard and often."

"Oh well," said Shane, "better luck next time."

"There's no next time for that bird—he's harder to lick than a champion—and he might lick a champion, and I'm goin' to be the world's champion."

Shane remembered his last fight with Garcia, and wondered until, rubbed down, he left the building with Jack Gill and his manager.

"Come along to Chicago with us," said Gill, "we've got two weeks in burlesque."

"Nope—I don't like burlesque."

"But you won't have to see it, Sap—you'll be workin' with me."

"Nope, Jack, I'm headin' for Omaha."

"All right—say hello to Buck Logan out there for me—that guy's heart's in the right place."

"Another fellow told me about him—Mankerlitz out of Phoenix."

"So you know Mank, do you—he's okeh—some good people in this racket—but don't miss Logan. He's worth a round trip. He was a fighter when he was a kid. He knows what it is to get belted around. Get him to talkin' sometime. You know a lot of them writin' saps are mighty dumb—they think because they can string words together they got the world by the tail, when all the time it's got them. But they wouldn't know what to do with a coupla cracks on the jaw. Everybody's got somethin', Kid—even that manager of mine —but I ain't found out what it is—but go to Logan— he's the bishop of us guys. He hears all our confessions. Get him to tell you about the time he fought the dinge in Winnipeg—and how he said to his second, 'Throw in the towel, I'm retirin' from the fray'—and the second says, 'That wasn't a hard wallop you took— just think what Battlin' Nelson would take'—and Buck says—'Well, Nelson would have quit had he took that one—you fight the next round—I'm through—' Well, so long, Shane—drop me a line any time, care of the *Chicago Tribune*—you're damn good people—you shoot square dice."

His green silk shirt wide open at the throat, his muscles bulging the shoulders, the wind blowing through his hair, Gill sat at the wheel. His manager climbed in beside him. The rear seat of his powerful car was loaded with many traveling bags. The car roared in the direction of Chicago.

Shane watched the luxurious sixteen-cylindered car until it faded from sight.

He was lonesome for Gill. He had learned a lot from him. He remembered his saying,

"You're the best man in the camp, Kid—don't you never forget it. You're growin' or I'd have to fight you some day—and I'd hate that—you might lick me—and if I was mad enough to lick you I'd be sorry."

Gill had never taken a drink in his life—had never used tobacco— "I just didn't—that's all."

The words impressed Shane.

"I wanta meet you again, Jack."

"We will—it's in the cards—if it ever comes rough, let me know."

"You're a pal, Jack."

"I like you, that's all—you take it and lash it out—and you don't whimper—a guy who can tear Maley to pieces is aces up with me—and I've never heard you say a word about it."

III

Shane never had so much money before. Remembering Gill's swagger and the powerful car, he walked about the streets of Wichita.

The lad who had bought trinkets in Mexico City that he did not need was soon buying a large wardrobe trunk and loading it with clothes.

He took a Pullman out of Wichita.

It was filled with men who had attended the convention.

All wanted to entertain the conqueror of Gunner Maley.

Shrewd men, who had gone far in the world, they had not learned what Shane and Gill knew by instinct —to be temperate with food and liquor.

To their amazement they observed that he who had been brutal as a strong wind against Maley was now bashful and awkward in his plush surroundings.

"I'd give a million to be in your shape," a bloated man said, "I wish you'd take me in hand. Too much flesh is like too much money—it makes you tired to carry it around."

"I wouldn't know about that," Shane returned unconsciously.

The rich man smiled. "You're a nice fellow. I thought fighters had horns."

"We need 'em," Shane said.

Reaching Omaha, he made his way to Buck Logan.

"Sure, Jack Gill wired me about you—so you got Maley in a round, huh—good work—I'll bet that Gill carried his man—he's a fox—lot of brains. Well, you oughta stay here a while. I'll smoke you up for some good matches."

"Another fellow wanted me to see you."

"Who's that?"

"Joe Mankerlitz—Phoenix."

"Oh yeah—he did write me about you—that's been some time ago—a good fellow, Joe—shady as a woods—but a honey if he's on your side."

Buck Logan had an immense head, large ears, square teeth, and bulging eyes. His body, once muscular, was now flabby. His delicate hands belied the rest of his body. His short fingers tapered. He wore thick glasses, against which his eyelashes rubbed. A wrinkle of neck fell over his collar.

Around sixty, his hair was thick gray.

He peered at Shane.

"What do you weigh—about 165—you'll fill out yet —you've got the frame for a heavyweight. Come up and see me any time. Where you staying? Better go to the Avon—nice quiet place—I'll get you set there— twelve a week. It pays to look flush. If people think you're in the money they give you more—unless you're a newspaperman—then all hell won't give you any money."

Through Logan's influence he was matched with Barney McCoy at a "smoker" given by the Elks Lodge.

He won the decision. The verdict helped make him a "card" in Omaha.

A match with Blinky Miller in Council Bluffs followed.

"He's supposed to be Eddie Turner from Chicago—but he's a ringer," Buck Logan explained. "You can take him. I'll use it after you lick him—it's a better story."

A "ringer" was a successful pugilist who used an assumed name and wagered money on himself against a less able bruiser.

After he knocked Miller out, Shane went to his dressing-room.

"You can hit, my boy," said Miller, rubbing his jaw, "You surprised me— I'm clean as a whistle—bet my whole end of the purse."

"Here's a hundred," said Shane.

The defeated fighter took the money. "Thanks, Pal, I'll remember this—I'm Blinky Miller."

"Sure," smiled Shane, "I was on from the first."

By a quirk of compassion, Buck Logan did not use the story. A rival paper told of Miller's identity.

Miller called on Buck.

"Thanks, Buck—you're real people. You can't blame me for losin' to that boy. I knew the first round I was up against it. He cracked me on the jaw so hard it was like someone run a sword in my ear. It was lucky I lasted as long as I did. I bet everything I had on myself."

"That's tough," said Logan, "Can I help?"

"No—the kid comes to my dressin' room and kicks in a hundred."

"Who—Rory?" exclaimed Logan.

"Sure—it come near knockin' me out agin—those things ain't done this year."

Buck wiped his heavy glasses. "Well I'll be damned." His eyes roved the clutter of the room. "He's a dead right kid—got all the right instincts."

"He can fight like hell too—" Blinky Miller added.

"Yeah—the poor devil—I hope he don't go the way all you guys go—it's like Spider Smith used to say—"

Shane greeted Logan. "Here's your enemy," the writer said.

"Hello," he shook Miller's hand.

"Blinky just told me a nice thing you did."

"Who—me?" Shane stammered.

"Yes, it was a damn nice thing," said Miller.

Shane frowned at him for silence.

Sensing the situation, Logan cut in, "You remember Spider Smith—don't you, Blinky?"

"Sure thing," answered Miller.

"I wonder whatever became of him?"

"God knows," returned Miller, "He's faded out somewhere."

Shane remained silent.

Buck Logan called to an assistant at the next desk. "Get Joe Watkins—we want a picture of this Damon and Pythias—for my collection—not for the paper—it might look bad."

Joe Mankerlitz came on from Phoenix as the manager of Barney McCoy.

"Give us a break for old times' sake, Shane—let Barney get a draw with you. It'll be all right with Buck when he gets back—there's room for us all—you can make it a fast go—just don't knock him out. You've beat him once—we both know you can do it again."

He had a more important match in Sioux City.

"You're on your way up," Buck Logan had said before leaving for New York to report a fight between Jerry Wayne and Bud Fealy.

It might have been different had a telegram not reached him from Jack Gill. Buck Logan died of heart failure on the train.

Since boyhood, death had not touched Shane. He was fond of Logan. For hours the sports' editor would sit at a corner table in "The Rendezvous" and tell him tales of the ring.

Shane's cockiness in the ring, his bashfulness outside, had appealed to Logan. He became his constant companion.

The table was often surrounded by newspapermen. He would listen to their talk with deep attention.

Logan's assistant was Ted Braly.

"I've got an idea, Ted. I wanta do something for Buck. Suppose we start a collection. I'll lead it off with a coupla hundred—he's got an aunt—she might need something."

"No, Shane—Buck's okeh—he had some money—the only thing you can do for him is carry him in your heart."

He was still depressed when Mankerlitz came to his hotel.

"Buck'll understand wherever he is," said Mankerlitz.

Shane consented to let McCoy stay the limit.

He realized too late that he was double-crossed. He lost the decision to McCoy—who replaced him on the card in Sioux City.

He remembered Logan's words about Mankerlitz— "shady as a woods."

He pleaded for a return match.

"I'd like to give it to you, Shane—but you know how it is—you can't blame Barney and me for makin' the most of things. Another win now over you wouldn't help us none—we're movin' out of here for a while."

The full force of his predicament came to Shane.

"So that's it, huh."

"Sure, Shane—that's it—you oughta knowed better." Joe Mankerlitz was not unkind. He laughed quietly.

The memory of Buck Logan and his own chagrin made him leave Omaha. The double-cross embittered him for weeks. He never again took the word of another in the ring.

IV

For several months Shane was too indifferent to seek matches. He had two thousand dollars, a large diamond ring, a half dozen silk robes, many suits of clothes, three trunks, and two watches.

As a road kid he had seen railroad employees look at watches of an expensive make. He paid a hundred dollars for one. "It's a twenty-five year gold case and twenty-one jewels," the salesman said.

"I know," returned Shane, putting the money on the glass case.

All found their way to pawn shops. He had paid five hundred for the ring. "A diamond's as good as money any day," the jeweler explained when he bought the bauble.

He pawned it for sixty dollars. "No more of these damn things for me," he said to the pawnbroker.

"Sixty dollars is better than no money," the dealer in lost vanity said.

"But it's not as good as five hundred," Shane pocketed the money.

"Look at the fun you had wearin' it." The pawnbroker looked at the stone.

He reached Cheyenne a year later where Jackie Connors, a one time bantamweight, was promoting fights.

"I'd like to fight Barney McCoy," he said to Connors.

The shriveled little promoter looked at Shane. "Just why McCoy?"

"Well, we'd draw some money— I licked him once, and he licked me, and it's not too far from Omaha."

"Are them the only reasons?"

"No—he put the double-o on me."

"He's goin' like a house afire now, you know," said the manager shrewdly.

"All right—all I want's expenses if I don't lick him—his manager'll think I'm a cinch now—and you can slip the word along I'm a set-up— Look here—" Shane handed a package of newspaper clippings to Connors.

"That's all right—I know you're a fighter," said Connors.

"Thanks—you don't know nothin' if you ain't seen me go. I carried that guy like a sap. My second kept sayin' that he was edgin' up on me—and I went clear screwy when the referee raises his hand—believe me, from now on I wouldn't even trust Jesus on a white horse."

"How long you been fightin'?" asked Connors.

"Oh, I don't know—three years maybe."

"I used to battle some myself."

"I know that—and you were good—you licked Willy Forbes, didn't you?"

"Yeap—got him in four—a good man, Willy."

"He musta been—got killed later, didn't he?"

"Yeap—One Round Riley got him—it was bad luck

—canvas wasn't padded where he went down. He died from concussion of the brain."

"Gee," from Shane.

"The racket ain't what it used to be," the one-time bantamweight commented.

"No, I guess not," returned Shane, "But do I get this fight— I'm right here, you know—you don't have to bring a guy in—you can tell the papers you sent for me from Chicago—you know—smoke it up—a grudge fight—then sneak it over to McCoy's gang I'm all through—you know how—"

The wrinkled promoter chuckled.

"You're tellin' me how—why, I was throwin' leather before you could crawl."

"I know that, and you were good, I know, but I can fight some. I wanta square things up with Buck Logan."

"He's dead," said Connors.

"Not for me he ain't dead—he's just as alive as I am." Shane patted his heart. "I can feel his eyes on me— 'You get McCoy'—and Buck Logan's ghost can strangle me if I don't win."

"All right." The weazened promoter looked Shane up and down, "I'm goin' to put you on with McCoy— Pioneer Day's a month off— I'll fix you up—leave it to me—you might even get a grand out of it—but you know—McCoy's better than he was—he beat Slippery Markowitz."

"So'd I—"

"All right, Buddy—I'll take you over to the Good Luck Restaurant so you kin scoff."

"That suits me."

Shane kept pace with Connors, who said, "There's a little dame over there. She's kinda sweet on me"—he looked at Shane's physique— "She's nuts about fighters, and she may go for you—but that's okey. I play the field—they're doin' me a favor when they don't marry me. I wouldn't hold her if I was big as John L. Sullivan."

"What's her name?"

"Interested, huh," Connors grimaced crookedly. "It's a funny name—Dilly Dally—last name's real, so her mother called her Dilly."

"Kind of cute." Shane stepped faster.

"Wait'll you see her." Connors kept pace. "Tell her you've been in Hollywood. She'll go for that—she's crazy to get in the movies."

Facing the depot was a restaurant. Above the door was painted a large red, white, and blue horse-shoe. Beneath were the words, "Good luck."

Connors opened the door.

"Hello there, Jackie," said Dilly.

Shane followed.

The girl stared.

"Brought along a pal of mine, Dilly. He fights here in about a month."

"Really—" her eyes opened.

"Yeap—agin Barney McCoy."

"Is that so?" Her eyes were still on Shane.

"Yeap—." Connors looked at one and then the other, much as a referee would at two pugilists. "Dilly Dally—meet Shane Rory."

She bowed politely and made an affected gesture. Shane nodded. "Glad to know you."

"He'll be eatin' here right along now—tell the boss I'm good for it."

"Oh, that's okeh." Dilly smiled. Her teeth were even as pearls in a row, her eyes large and brown, her hair tinged with gold. Her close-fitting waist, open low at the throat, revealed the form of her breasts.

As they seated themselves, she leaned over Shane and said, "What'll it be?" Her breast touched Shane's shoulder.

"Give us both some ham and eggs, coffee and toast," Connors spoke quickly.

"All right." She stepped gracefully to the kitchen. Their eyes followed.

"Could you go for that?" Connors grinned crookedly at Shane.

"I'll say—any time. She's beautiful."

Connors' voice rose. "She is beautiful—that kid'll get some place just as sure's a preacher goes to church on Sunday."

When she returned, Connors said, "Be nice to Shane here, won't you, Dilly—he'll have to be in good shape to lick McCoy."

Dilly placed the food on the table. "Sure I'll be nice to him." She touched his shoulder. "I'll bet McCoy won't get no place fast with him—I know a good man when I see one."

"That's more'n most women do," chuckled Connors.

"Well, I'm not *most women*."

"That's right, Dilly—you don't belong in Cheyenne."

Shane's eyes did not leave her.

"How long you been here?" he asked.

"Too long," was the answer, "I've only got fifty-one more years if I live my full time out. I've spent forty of them here."

"You've only been here four months," put in Connors.

"Well, that's forty years the way I figure."

All three laughed.

"It won't seem so long if you're nice to him here." Connors nodded toward Shane.

"I'll be nice. I don't have to have a brick house fall on me to take the hint." She looked at Shane. "Will you take me to see you fight?"

"Sure."

"I'll be prayin' for you," she said. "Do you want your coffee now?"

"Yes, please," returned Shane.

"Mine later, Sis," said Connors.

"Take it easy," he cautioned Shane, as she left. "Don't fall too hard for a dame in a railroad restaurant."

In spite of Connors' warning, Shane was infatuated with Dilly. For the next few weeks she saw no one else.

Her home was in Grand Island, Nebraska. She was working her way to Hollywood. "I've had a lot of chances to go," she explained to Shane, "but I wanta get there honorable—I don't wanta lot of strings on me."

"Why not let's go to Frisco after the fight—I'll have six or eight hundred dollars."

"How far's that from Hollywood?" she asked.

"Oh, about five hundred miles—I'd send you down —the game's good in Frisco. I'll get by McCoy, then I'll be a card."

"Just think," she said admiringly, "all that money in one night. Gee, you must be smart. I'd sling hash a year for that much."

"Well, it's different," Shane was earnest, "All I've got to have is a strong jaw and a weak mind."

"Your mind's not so weak, dear." Her hand touched the muscle of his arm. "It would be nice to leave here —you know how it is—you can't turn sideways in a town like this but what they'll talk about you—and a girl can't stay home all the time twiddlin' her thumbs."

"That's right," agreed Shane.

"It wouldn't be so bad, but I have to send my step-father money. He's not much good, but my mother used to like him before she died."

"That's too bad—I mean," Shane was confused.

"That's right—it was too bad—she done everything for him—but that's the way it goes. If you don't kick a man first, he will you."

"That's right," Shane agreed.

With such talk, the hours passed.

She would hold his hand in the movies, and sigh at

the tribulations of the heroine. The love scenes en-thralled her. Above the silence her breath would come quickly.

Intent on the coming fight and vengeance, the days flew swiftly. The wind purring the sand down the streets of Cheyenne did not sound lonely to him. Dilly Dally was in town.

"Now listen, Shane," Connors said two days before the fight, "I've tried to steer you right—don't go nuts on that kid. She's smart as salt in a fresh cut. Never trust a dame in a railroad restaurant. She's too purty. Have all the fun you want—but don't get that calf look in your eyes. I'm not sayin' anything against her—it's not that—I used to have a bird dog. If anybody picked up a gun around it, it'd go nuts—it couldn't help it—it was anybody's dog who'd go huntin'."

"You don't mean she's not on the square?"

"Now, what would you think—she took me for a hundred before I got next—said the baby was mine."

"I don't believe you—you're kiddin'," said Shane.

The talk still worried him.

"You've never done nothin' wrong in this town, have you, Dilly?"

Her eyes raised. "I should say not—nor no other town—we've been together a long time—*I'm straight with you and I like you.*" She became fretful. "I just knew they'd talk about me if I ever met some boy I liked." Her eyes were tearful.

Shane was ashamed.

"Now don't let on to anybody—we can get out of

here when the fight's over—when I do find the man I love, that'll be different."

"Is it me?"

She huddled close. "Can't you guess?"

Shane looked straight ahead and saw nothing.

He was in his dressing-room while the first preliminary was being fought.

Two men entered without knocking.

He was carefully rolling the tape over his knuckles.

"Hello there, Rory," said the heavier man. "You look in good shape—how long's the fight gonna last?"

"Oh," Shane shrugged, "you can't tell—he's a good boy—anything can happen in there."

"That's what we wanta talk to you about—to keep the record clear—you understand."

"What's there to understand?"

"Plenty," was the answer. "You're a good-lookin' kid—we don't even know where your mother lives—if you've got one—and we don't wanta be mean and send you to her in a box—"

The heavier man fondled a revolver.

"I get it," said Shane. "You're on McCoy to win."

"That's it."

"McCoy's got to win, huh."

"You guessed it again. The bank roll's on him."

"Why can't we make it a nice draw?"

"We can't use a draw—it's got to be a knockout."

Shane loosened his shoulder muscles. "Connors has been good to me—I promised him a good fight for this chance—you wouldn't want me to let him down."

"Well, it's too bad—but there's no way out."

"Well, I guess you've got me—give me five or six rounds."

"Seven's the limit."

"All right."

As Shane entered the ring he glanced through the ropes at the gamblers. Each had his right hand in a coat pocket.

Neither fighter spoke when receiving instructions. Rory went forward slowly at the gong, moving his gloved left hand up and down a few inches, his eyes narrow, his chin buried. A full minute passed. Each time McCoy led, his opponent stepped aside. Suddenly Rory stepped in. McCoy was between him and the gamblers. Rory's left shoulder was low. McCoy's chin might have been fastened on it. Rory's right moved three times, not over eight inches, trip-hammer fashion.

McCoy's jaw went sideways. His eyes turned glass. His mouth flew open. He fell as suddenly as a shot bull.

Men stood dumfounded about the ring. The count over, Rory went to his dressing-room without looking in the direction of the gamblers.

V

Shane watched the sea gulls fly on the wharf at San Francisco. Dilly Dally had left for Hollywood with the last hundred dollars. Eight hundred had gone in four weeks.

It was time to fight again.

He thought over his life, and wondered about Buck Logan and Spider Smith. His fights with Barney Mc-Coy returned.

It was sunny weather. The white clouds moved slowly in a blue sky across the bay.

Jackie Connors was right about Dilly. She had told him everything. "I think we'd better bust up," she said. "I ain't worthy of a boy like you—maybe some day I will be."

"Well—that's that," he said. "So long."

"You won't be mad, will you, dear?"

"Who—me—what at? We've both got to get by. I've got to get me some fights. There's nothing doin' here."

It had been pleasant, he remembered.

He did not feel hurt at her confession. People could only misuse him in the ring.

"You and me's different—I don't know why," she said one day as they wandered through Golden Gate Park. "I'm just made wrong—but I'll never forget you."

44

Spider Smith had talked about women in Mexico City. "The only way to get one dame outta your head's to get another one."

He did not understand. Girls had never bothered him—except one—a little. And then, he left because he did not want to be in the way.

Once, in a moment of confidence, he had told Dilly about her.

"So her pa owns a big farm," she sighed, her eyes narrow. "It's a good thing you left before he chased you."

She had not been the same since.

"Oh, well!"

Silent Tim Haney was in Portland. It was seven hundred miles away.

He had fourteen dollars left. He would have to beat his way.

In three days he was at the gymnasium of the Ideal Athletic Club.

It was crowded with fighters. Old timers, with broken noses, and ears like hunks of gristle, talked with lads still unmarked by the leather of the ring.

Silent Tim Haney was the manager of the gymnasium. He was also the matchmaker for the Ideal Athletic Club. He sat on a rickety chair in his green-painted, pine-board office. On the walls were pictures of fighters and women in tights. In the center of one group was a photograph of George Washington; of the other, Abraham Lincoln.

The manager was in a stormy mood. The directors had held a special meeting. Their object was to determine why the Ideal Athletic Club was losing money. "They ain't no more good fighters left," the manager wailed. The battered gathering of elemental ruffians nodded their heads in approval.

A knock came to the door. "Come on in, for God in Heaven's sake—this ain't a church."

It opened quickly. Shane Rory walked before him.

He carried a small, cheap, ancient handbag. Hatless, his hair straggled in all directions. He wore a faded blue serge suit, a green flannel shirt, and canvas shoes that had once been white.

"Mr. Haney," the husky young fellow put the bag on the floor in the manner of a bell boy, "My name's Shane Rory—I'd like to fight for you."

The manager and his gathering looked at the lad.

Shane's eyes were bloodshot. His chin was square and firm. His shoulders were thrown forward. In spite of many gloves, his nose was one a woman might envy.

"What's wrong with your eyes?" the manager asked.

"Nothin's wrong with my eyes," replied Shane.

"They're all red," said Silent Tim Haney.

"I got cinders in 'em. Been ridin' the blind baggage all night."

The manager moved his shoulders, "Road kid, huh."

"Yeap—I've been tourin' around—and I'm sick of it. I get a little dough—and I spend it in no time and I'm broke again—up and down all the time like an elevator—but I can fight—don't get me wrong. I've just been a sap. I'm on my way now— See these clippin's." He held a handful of newspaper items toward the manager.

"Any good men among 'em?"

"Plenty—see here—I licked Blinky Miller."

"Not *the* Blinky Miller—you wouldn't be on the bum now if you could do that." Silent Tim Haney's voice rose.

"Many a good man's been on the bum—and I'm not a liar—I licked Blinky Miller—it's all here in English —I broke his heart, Mr. Haney—you could hear it snap when I begun to get the range— If Buck Logan was alive he'd tell you plenty about me—if he'd of lived I'd be champion now. I was Jack Gill's sparring partner. I cracked Gunner Maley in the semi to him. You don't hear of him no more. I took Barney McCoy'n a round."

The manager became more alert.

"What name'd you fight under?" He still ignored the clippings.

"Wildcat Rory."

"Clawed 'em to death, huh—you talk like a champeen," the managed bantered. The gathering laughed aloud, as men will at a benefactor's humor.

The lad's eyes went to the circle of the bruisers, and returned to the manager.

"I told you," he said, "I wanted to fight for you."

"Any particular place on the bill? The top spot, I suppose," said Silent Tim Haney. Guffaws followed the manager's words.

When the laughter subsided, the boy answered slowly, "No place in particular, Mr. Haney. Any place'll do me." He stopped for a second, "And anybody, any size." His razor lips cut the last words. "You

remember the night I fought the semi to Jerry Wayne
—he says to me—'Boy, I'm glad I'm goin' and you're
comin''— I liked Jerry after that—he knew I'da took
him in a coupla more years—it took a big guy to
admit that."

The manager attempted to remember.

"Was that on Old Settlers' Day?"

"Yes, sir—Jerry Wayne won in four rounds—and I
won in one."

"So you think you'd of took Jerry, huh?"

"Well, we're sayin' nothin' now about them that's
worse than dead, for it can't be proved ever—but don't
let these palookers around here laugh you outta seein'
me go—all you'll ever get outta these stumble bums
is the holes in the doughnuts." He shoved his right
hand quickly through his tangled hair, and looked
scornfully around.

"What do you weigh?" asked the manager.

"A hundred and sixty-eight, stripped."

"Wanta put on the gloves with anybody here?"
The manager looked about.

"Anybody," snapped the boy.

"Get Harry Sully," commanded the manager, "we'll
see how good you are."

Harry Sully, just becoming a prominent heavyweight, came into the room.

"He's got it on you twenty pounds, but you don't
mind that, do you?" said the manager.

"Not atall," said Shane.

The manager, still by way of banter, "Are you sure
you kin be a card for me?"

Shane pointed to Harry Sully, "Ask him when we're through."

"Well, I'm looking for a new face to fight the main bout with him—see what you can do—"

"Well, I'm your huckleberry, Mr. Haney—I was born with my fists closed. They had to pry 'em open."

"Do you always brag this way?" said the manager.

"I don't brag, Mr. Haney. I've got to get off the bum. Besides, I may as well say it as think it—and I don't believe in lyin'—you can put it down in your little red notebook—I've been foolin' around with the gloves ever since I was seven years old."

He laid his clothes on an old chair. Standing nude, he jerked a pair of yarn tights from the handbag.

"Ain't you got no protectors—you're liable to get hit low."

The boy looked at the manager. "They can't hit low when they're busy backin' up," he said, "now can they, Mr. Haney?"

The manager's eyes opened in amazement.

"Do you know who Harry Sully is?" he asked.

"Sure I know who everybody is—does he know who I am—but anyhow, Mr. Haney—I always remembered you after Butte—I said to myself right then, 'Some day I'll team up with him.' I knew then you had your hands full with one good fighter—and *Jerry Wayne was good*."

"You admit it, eh?" said the manager, pleased.

"Sure—anyone could see that. I didn't dress till his fight was over that night—I just set in my bathrobe and watched him throw them gloves."

"Well, you watched a great man at his best." The manager's eyes lit with happy memory. "A machine gun couldn't throw gloves any faster."

"And his foot work," marveled Shane, "He could dance a jig on a dime."

"Yes, yes, indeed—a wonderful boy."

"I fought him and won," Harry Sully said, waiting.

"You fought his shadow," Silent Tim Haney said, without looking at Sully.

"That night in Butte," continued Shane, "you were up collectin' the money, I guess, Mr. Haney. I went to see Jerry after the fight, and I said to him, 'I think you got it on 'em all, Jerry,' and he puts his arm around me and says, 'You're not so bad yourself, Kid. I watched you in that one round— Snap your left more when you move in for the kill.' I never forgot that. I won my next fight with a short left. I always liked him after that—and I was sorry to hear he got beat."

He looked across at Harry Sully, who stood, frowning. Sully's shoulders were broad and stooped near to abnormal. Over six feet, he seemed shorter. His hair was clipped close. His nose was large and flat. His ears were small and out of shape. His jaw was undershot, long and square. Beginning at a hundred and thirty, he had fought at different weights. His greatest feat had been in whipping Jerry Wayne.

The gloves on, Shane began to bounce around and throw blows at an imaginary foe.

Harry Sully stepped jauntily toward him when the gong rang.

He was smothered in a flurry of blows. Unable to

keep the newcomer away from him with all his knowledge, he went to his corner at the end of the round with a surprised expression.

"I told Wilson I'd see that you got a good workout," Silent Tim Haney smiled.

When the gong sounded, Silent Tim looked at Sully and said, "Come on, Harry, this is the last round."

The youth was on top of him again. At the end of the round, he was still flailing with both gloves.

Silent Tim waited until Sully came to his corner.

"That kid's a wildcat," he grumbled.

Silent Tim hurried to Shane. "Where are you from?"

"No place."

"Been fightin' long?"

"Off an' on for quite a while—I never took it very serious—anything to make a livin'."

"Who was it you fought in Butte?"

"Eddie Flynn."

"Huh—a good boy." Tim Haney's manner changed. "I remember now." He looked around. "Well, you made good here. I'll give you a match with Sully. Al Wilson, his manager, wants me to get him a fight." He put his hand on Shane's shoulder. "Don't say nothin' to nobody—I may wanta manage you."

"It's all right with me," returned Shane, putting on his worn coat, and picking up the small handbag. "I'm sick of floatin' around."

"Where you livin'?" asked Mr. Haney.

"I don't know," replied Shane, "some little joint I

flopped in last night. Fellow from Loue-e-ville runs it—down on Post Street—here's his card."

The manager wrote the address.

"I'll be seein' you," he said, "an' remember, you're on in the main event a week from this comin' Saturday."

"All right—where'll I train?"

"I'll phone Lavin's and fix it up—it's only a little ways from where you stay."

"Okeh," returned Shane, as he left.

Silent Tim Haney returned to his rickety chair. For a moment he was silent, and stared at the picture of Abraham Lincoln.

Different stooges talked low. The young bruiser's personality still echoed in the room. It had the semi-quiet of a place just raided by the police.

"That guy's a storm, eh, Mr. Haney?" finally came from a stooge.

Silent Tim's eyes moved from George Washington to the picture of a slender woman in tights.

"I'll say he's a storm," cut in Harry Sully, now dressed—"gimme a cigarette somebody—he tried to lay me out— He kin hit."

"How'd you like to fight him?" Silent Tim Haney asked.

"Any time."

"He may take you." Silent Tim still stared at the lady in tights.

"That's what you thought about Jerry Wayne." Silent Tim turned suddenly, but said nothing. Sully blew a ring of smoke. "There's nobody lickin' me."

"How about Torpedo Jones?" Silent Jim snapped the question.

"Fluke decision—I'll knock that Nigger dead if he ever fights me again. I was born to lick him."

"I didn't see the fight," pursued Silent Tim, "but from what I hear you fought him wrong—tryin' to counter punch with him."

"I don't fight none of them palookas wrong—besides I beat him—you can ask my manager. Al Wilson'll tell you I had him woozy in the seventh."

"Maybe Al's prejudiced, bein' your manager."

"Who—Wilson prejudiced—you don't know that guy—to hear him talk you'd think I didn't have a chance with anybody. He's always jackin' me up like I was some stumble bum, an' not a comin' champeen."

Silent Tim, taunting, "It takes more'n nerve to be champeen, Sully—many are called, so the Good Book says, but very few are chosen."

"Well, I'm called—you hear that." Sully threw the cigarette from him. "You never give me a chance with Jerry Wayne," his voice raised, "If you'd had good ears you'd of heard me bein' called that night. You saw me whip Wayne—he was a *good man*."

"Again I tell you, you whipped a good man's shadow." Silent Tim's words were sharp.

"Shadow—hell—I kin whip an army of shadows like him."

"Quit talkin' about the dead," snapped Silent Tim.

"Mr. Haney's right," said a stooge—"let the dead rest."

"He ain't dead," sneered Sully.

Silent Tim remained pensive, while the stooge said, "He's the same as dead."

Sully snorted— "I know better—you're not foolin' me—he's in the bug-house."

"Go and fight Torpedo Jones again—he'll put you there." Silent Tim turned to the picture of Abraham Lincoln.

"Him and who else—they ain't no bug-house big enough to hold me."

Silent Tim's eyes returned to Sully. "You're right."

VI

When the directors of the Ideal Athletic Club learned that Shane Rory was matched with Harry Sully, they sent for Silent Tim Haney.

He stood before the directors.

"Who has he fought?" asked the chairman.

"A lot of good boys," answered the manager. He named several.

"Never heard of 'em," said the chairman.

"That don't mean nothin'. Lots of people never heard of Napoleon," returned Silent Tim Haney. "This boy's goin' places. He's got dynamite'n his gloves."

"We can't have the match," said the chairman.

"Then you can't have me neither. I'm quits unless he goes on. I got some dignity left. The guy's a murderer in the ring. He's liable to kill Sully."

"What are you givin' him?" asked a director.

"Four hundred."

The directors stood up.

"We can't have it! We can't have it!" they exclaimed in unison. "How can we show a profit, givin' preliminary boys money like that?"

Haney spoke swiftly.

"This boy's no preliminary fighter. He'll lick any man his weight in the world." Haney paused, "If you don't believe it, he'll tell you so himself." He became more earnest. "I don't go wrong on fighters—he's got something in his eyes. There's a blaze in his head. He's burnin' to go all the time. Leave it to me."

After a tirade of such talk, the chairman, fully convinced, but trying to hide it, drawled, "All right, Tim, but—we can't take a chance—Harry Sully'd knock him clear outta the ring."

"You think so," snorted Haney. "There ain't nobody knockin' this bozo out of the ring. You see him go once an' you'll swear he's got cyclones in his gloves. He blisters the air when he misses."

The chairman looked indifferent. His manner irritated Haney, who said tersely,

"I'll tell you what I'll do—if he don't lick Sully, *I'll kick in the four hundred.*"

"Oh well, we wouldn't have you do that," said the chairman with more warmth.

"The devil you wouldn't. Don't try to kid any old kidder like me." Silent Tim Haney frowned.

"Well—if you'd rather—we'll take your offer," returned the chairman.

"It's too late—I take it back," snapped Haney. "I'll make you another. If he don't win, he gets half of four centuries. If he does—he gets four hundred dollars."

The directors looked startled.

"It's a fair offer," said Haney. "If he licks Sully he's a card. If he don't—you'll see a great fight anyhow."

"But how can he expect to lick Sully?" asked a director. "And how do we know he's a great fighter?"

"I'm telling you he's a great fighter. Don't worry about what he's done before. Who was young Corbett till he knocked McGovern silly? He learned the game in the tanks whippin' a lot of mighty good men. There's not much difference between a first and second rater . . . lots of times it's as hard to lick one as the other. I've seen fighters wake up in the morning great fighters. Something happens to them. This kid's about found himself. I can tell."

"But we're not stickin' around till fighters wake up," a director said.

"Well, have it your way," returned Silent Tim, "I know more about this kid'n he thinks I do. I saw him belt Eddie Flynn out in less'n two minutes. Flynn might never be a champeen but he might lick a champeen—there's no palookas knockin' him over—it takes a hell of a good man to lick another good man in two minutes."

"Maybe he got him cold," said the chairman.

"Cold or hot," Silent Tim came back, "not till you've been in there will you ever know how hard and swift a punch or how good a man it takes to knock a fighter like Flynn over. Ketchell popped up over night, didn't he? And he was always a great fighter."

"Who else did Rory lick?" asked the chairman.

"Blinky Miller for one—knocked him bow-legged. He sat down like a Buddha an' rolled over."

"Not *the* Blinky Miller?" two directors asked.

"Yeap—that's him—I don't want Wilson to know that—he won't throw Sully in with a boy who can punch hard enough to drop Miller."

"Who else did he lick?"

"Barney McCoy and Gunner Maley—he got 'em in a round like he did Flynn."

The chairman looked at the clock. "All right, Tim —it's on—we have confidence in you."

"Shake," said Haney.

On the night of the fight, Shane Rory skipped down the aisle with a ragged bath-towel thrown across his shoulders.

The open air building was cold. He worked his feet deep into the resin box in one corner of the ring and drew the towel about him.

Shane's second patted his shoulder as the referee called the fighters to the center of the ring.

"He's built like a brick barn," a ringsider said, glancing at Rory's slender waist and wide shoulders.

"You mean a tiger," said another.

Smooth as still water, Shane's muscles were without bulge. He walked as though highly resilient rubber were in his heels.

Sully, a red silk robe on his well-conditioned body, looked indifferently at his adversary, and then at the canvas floor. The audience cheered.

Both pugilists nodded approval of the instructions.

The gong sounded.

Silent Tim Haney watched from a ringside seat while the fighters maneuvered for openings.

None came during the first round.

After the bell rang for the second, Sully butted Rory.

There was a deep cut above his eye. His second tried to talk to him during the minute's rest.

"I'm fightin' this fight," he said, "I'll knock him back in the dollar seats before I'm through."

The bell clanged.

Shane's head was down. Sully ripped a right from his toes. It caught Shane on the chin. He rolled with the punch; then charged. It was as if a tiger sprang.

Sully's body turned red under the thunder of blows. He sank and got up again.

Shane was on his toes, sizzling murderous punches. All hit their target. Sully sagged, and backed away from the fusillade. Rory tore in, his lips set, his eyes narrowed.

When the round ended, Sully was across the ropes. His seconds hurried to him.

When the fourth round came, the applause had not subsided. Men stood upon their seats.

Sully was not through.

His blood-soaked glove ripped upward. Rory went down. At the count of eight, he saw men fly through the air, carrying their chairs with them.

At nine he was up. Sully was upon him.

Blows cracked, swift as bullets. They stood in close. Under the merciless pounding, Sully crumpled and rolled over three times.

He was up before the count of ten, and charging Shane, head downward. The wound above Shane's eye bled profusely.

His seconds were unable to stop the flow of blood between rounds.

The referee looked at the deep wound and awarded the fight to Sully.

"Thank God," groaned Al Wilson.

Shane sneered in his corner. "They're a lot of sissies —afraid of a little blood."

"It's for the good of the game," soothed Silent Tim Haney. "You oughta be glad you made such a showin'."

"Huh," grunted Shane, "you ain't never seen a good fighter."

Silent Tim was abashed in the presence of such confidence. Before he recovered from his surprise, Shane added, "I kin live on turnips and lick stumble bums like him."

"It's tough he cut your eye open," said Silent Tim Haney.

"Why should that make any difference—I kin lick him blind—and here I'm loser—I'm gettin' out of here tomorrow."

Silent Tim took Shane to his small hotel.

When he called the next day, Shane had gone.

VII

A barrel-shaped man, Silent Tim moved in his rough world without friction. His iron-gray hair was straight as wire. Gentle on the surface and never flustered, he early discovered that honeyed words were harder to dispute. He would often lapse into brogue.

"It's too bad he never gets a break—he's got a big brain," was Wild Joe Ryan's opinion of him. Wild Joe was a jewelry salesman whose hobby was pugilism. His entire world consisted of characters connected with the ring. Wherever a national contest was held, Wild Joe Ryan was among those present. About as wild as Tim Haney was silent, he had carried the nickname for years. He talked of ring dignitaries with deep respect. His conversation was full of such phrases as "Tex Rickard says to me," and "I says to Jim Corbett—"

One of his shoulders was lower than the other.

He arrived in town some time after the Sully fight.

Deferential to Tim Haney, as one of the kings of his world, he now approached him. After the greeting, he said quickly,

"Saw a boy down South who's a comer, Tim."

In the course of many wandering years, Wild Joe Ryan had told Silent Tim of many such comers. They were never heard of again.

Thinking of Shane Rory, his heart beating swiftly, Tim said indifferently—

"Didya—who?"

Wild Joe Ryan fumbled in his pocket and brought out a piece of paper. Adjusting his nose glasses that dangled from a black string, he read for a minute; then said, "His name's Rory—Shane Rory—he's built like Bob Fitzsimmons—only better legs—big shoulders, slender hips—fast as hell and a killer—I saw him at a smoker the Elks gave—the boys thought they'd entertain me a little. After seein' him go, I thought of you right away."

"Kin he box?" Tim asked warily.

"Yes—but that's not what impressed me, Tim. He kin take it and give it—his jaw's so sharp it'd cut the leather of a glove. He's a good-lookin' boy—"

"To hell with that," snapped Tim.

"I don't mean it just that way, either—everybody likes him down there—he hardly ever talks, he don't smoke or chase around with women."

Wild Joe Ryan removed his glasses and said decisively, "If I knew the fight game like you do, Tim, I'd sink everything I had on him—he's got it, I tell you—he must weigh a hundred and seventy or eighty now, and he'll still fill out—he's fast as a lightweight—and he hits like a mule kickin'."

Wild Joe Ryan snapped his fingers quickly— "He was up against a big, fast coon when I saw him, and he knocked him sideways and backwards so fast the Nigger didn't know which way to fall—it took two men to get that black man's jaws back in place after he come to—"

Silent Tim Haney showed no surprise, as he asked, "What kind of a punch?"

"I don't know," returned Wild Joe Ryan, "he cracked him so fast nobody could see where it come from."

"What was you drinkin'?" asked Tim.

Wild Joe Ryan was slightly irritated.

"All I'm doin' is telling you where to find a million dollars in a hick town—that's all I'm doin'." He looked at Silent Tim Haney. "I'm telling you this, Tim, because we're pals—we've known each other thirty-odd years." He fingered his noseglasses, "And I know you're on the level."

"Most certainly," replied Tim indignantly, "What town's he in?"

"Buffington."

"I'll be seein' you soon, Joe," said Silent Tim Haney.

Haney arrived in Buffington.

A group of young fellows, among them Shane, were in a small gymnasium.

Unaware that a one-time great pugilist watched them through a hole in the building, they went through different exercises.

At last Shane boxed. He was now calm, where he had been a charging fury against Sully. He landed punches without effort. His opponent could not touch him. The gymnasium shook.

An unconscious master of melodrama, Tim visualized him in a ring surrounded by howling thousands. Primitive as the first religion, and cunning as the first lie, Tim felt more elated than a miser discovering gold.

His heart pumped with the ancient lure of battle. He felt the cleft in his jaw that many fists had battered. He stood in the office of Madison Square Garden making demands on manager and directors.

"But this boy'll turn 'em away a mile down Broadway," he was saying to himself. "Give him a pat on the back between rounds and he kin lick all the heavyweights alive."

Shane, without a rest, began to punch the bag.

When all was over and the boys had dressed, he walked slowly away. Tim followed him.

Shane turned. Startled, he said, "You!"

"Yes—I got lonesome to see you." Tim coughed. "I'd like to sign you to a contract."

"Why didn't you think of that before I fought Sully?"

"I did, but you left town too quick," was the answer. "I had a return match for you with Harry Sully."

"When?" Shane asked.

Tim thought quickly. "Three weeks from now—the club's lined up till then."

"How'd you happen to find me here?" asked Shane.

"I read about you knockin' a Nigger out."

Silent Tim looked about. "Got any relations here?"

"None—I'm like a crow—I've no relations no place," replied Shane.

"Thank God for that," snapped Silent Tim. "You're

a wild horse," he continued. "You'll tear yourself to pieces and get nowhere on the track—the steam in the engine, and the lightning in the sky—it's no good if you don't control it. Stick with me and I'll get you in the big money. It don't hurt any more to get beat up for a million than it does for a dollar."

"I don't know—I never got beat up for a million."

"But you will if you stick with me," Silent Tim added.

"All right, you do the matchin' and I'll do the fightin'."

"Shake," said Tim— "I just want your word—it's fifty-fifty all the way. I'll pay hotel expenses out of my end."

"That's a go," agreed Shane.

Silent Tim smiled, and glanced at him with keen eyes. He could tell a better-than-average pugilist at once—the drawn skin, the muscles without bulge, the easy movement of body. He noted that Shane's knees were close together, that he stood with his feet apart, unconsciously prepared to balance himself against the blows of an adversary.

"Come on, my boy, let's go back and fight Harry Sully—I can get you five centuries."

"All right," agreed Shane.

"Then when you win, I'll quit everything and look after you."

"You'd better," said Shane, "A club like that never saw a real fighter."

VIII

Silent Tim Haney had but one ambition, to develop and manage a heavyweight champion. Close contact with the ring since boyhood had taught him its devious ways.

He had survived twenty years as a bruiser. He would study an adversary as a general would a map. Loquacious, thin-lipped, sardonic, he laid the gloves aside only when his knees began to creak. He spent hours each day trying to strengthen them.

Unusual in that he was a great manager who had also been a great pugilist, he was the only man who ever whipped Joe Slack. They were never friends afterward.

His four fights with Slack were memorable in ring annals. Knowing that his manager had absconded with his end of the purse, Tim won the last grueling contest with Slack.

The promoter wanted to pay his expenses.

"No, it was worth it to lick Slack."

"Well, we'll find your friend for you and make him give you the money."

Silent Tim retorted, "No—a friend who'll steal your money is not worth finding."

When the manager was located later, Tim refused to prosecute.

He had a profound knowledge of the human body

under strain. He knew that a great heavyweight pugilist came but seldom among millions of men. Three times he had been near the goal when the protégé developed some weakness. The Dublin Slasher was greatest of all. He died early. Eddie Curran might also have been a heavyweight champion had he been born five years later. He could whip the reigning champion—had done it convincingly in a no-decision fight. There was only one barrier in his way. He could not whip Billy Hill, a second-rate pugilist, after three attempts. The champion, afraid of the Slasher, when pressed to give him a fight, referred to his record with Hill. The latter had fought the champion and by so doing had proved that the man with the title did not belong in the same ring with him. Tim cursed his bad luck in matching his man with Hill, and concluded that guiding a man to a heavyweight championship was more delicate than assembling a watch.

Persuasive as good news, Tim was unctuous with men who wrote about pugilism for the daily papers. His anecdotes were many, and always had a laugh at the end.

Sensing early that in the heart of every newspaper writer was the seed of defeat, he tinged his flattery with humility. He would say of what they wrote, "I wish I had written that." He had never, so far as men knew, read beyond the headlines and the first paragraph.

He would inveigle men into telling stories. Though his mind might be far away, he would nod his head at certain points, as if listening intently.

Knowing Shane had great possibilities, Silent Tim Haney's chief idea in training him was for strength and endurance. Already an excellent boxer, he would absorb everything else. Trotting and walking rapidly, with occasional sprints, Shane went fourteen miles a day on soft country roads to avoid "shin splints."

The average pugilist ran five miles.

For an hour he would use the light bag for speed, hitting it with accurate precision. The larger bag was used for punching power. Blows were delivered against it, hard enough to knock a horse down. He was always "on his toes" in the gymnasium, even when wrestling the immense sand bag. He would skip a rope to develop fast foot work. He would lie flat on the floor and raise up from the waist, often lifting a weight as he did so. He would stretch out across a chair, hooking his legs under another chair upon which Silent Tim would sit and give ballast.

It was long, tiresome and relentless labor. If it ever tired the young fighter, he said nothing. He entered the gymnasium with the same zest each day.

A contraption of leather pads pounded his stomach until it was a mass of writhing muscle.

Tim watched Shane closely in the gymnasium and pointed out errors. "It's well I know that a man with never a glove on might whip you, but it's best to know more than other men anyhow."

He was satisfied that Shane knew instinctively how to hit.

A blow from him, traveling six inches, "in close," and unperceived, could knock an opponent unconscious. He could "throw" a blow that distance as swiftly as one would fire a shot. In delivering an "uppercut," he would "lift" his body with the punch. It was like being struck with a sledge his weight. Men who did not know how to put their weight behind blows were called "arm hitters."

He could not explain his movements in the ring. Mind and muscle coördinated so evenly that one seemed to work as quickly as the other.

He averted blows by the imperceptible movement of the head. He "rolled with the punch" or was "going away" when it was delivered, thus breaking its force.

His judgment of distance was acquired by hours of practice. At the zenith of a whirling fray, he seldom missed.

"Watch lions, leopards, and tigers when they're ready to spring. They'll teach you how to attack," said Tim. "And clinch as little as possible. That wears you out. You'll seldom knock a good man like Sully out with one punch. It may take ten—all dynamite. You've got to be in a position to slam them in when you get an opening. If you throw your body forward with all you've got and miss, you either fall into a clinch or into a counter-sock. If you do hit and then clinch, you give your opponent time to recuperate, and he may tire you. Most fighters are maulers, always clinching and off balance."

He shifted his feet with different punches.

When he struck, he would step in with one foot and hold the other back as an anchor. He was always within hitting range. "Don't lean over to reach your mark—

that throws you off balance," Tim reminded him.

Shane would make his left foot firm for leverage in driving a left-hand punch home, then move the right leg forward to give him balance for a right-hand blow. This enabled him to shuffle in with a balanced attack. In fast action he could punch straight or hook with either fist without drawing back a muscle. This was "snapping his punches," the weight of his body behind them.

"You may know what *you're goin'* to do—the trick is to make the other fellow do what you want him to," said old Tim often. "If your brain's trained well it'll work better when the fast fighters throw them at you a thousand a minute. You may think you forget—but you don't. You can make everything else even in the world but men's brains in the ring."

Silent Tim had learned too late how to hit without injuring his hand. He passed the knowledge on to Shane. When hitting, he turned his fist so the thumb was downward.

To feint with a right and hit with a left, though seeming simple, was difficult to learn.

A pugilist who only charged and hit "in close" was soon helpless and "out of position" before Shane. He would step aside, catch his arms, and spin him around quickly. Before the man could gain his equilibrium, he was knocked to the canvas with zipping "one-twos" to the jaw.

To counter a swinging right hand, he would swerve under and snap a vicious right to his opponent's heart or solar plexus.

Before a "body puncher," he would hold his arms close to his sides and counter with short snapping jolts to the chin.

He would get "the range" on a fast-moving target by "feeling" out with an open left glove. If this were not possible in the first few rounds, he would "slow him up" with hard, body punches by shuffling inside his guard. Whenever he touched his opponent's body with the end of his left glove, he would crash at the slowing target with his right. If the opponent went "in a shell" behind his left, with a right ready, Shane would "throw left hands."

"There's a defense for every lead," Silent Tim insisted. "The only trick in counter-punchin' is to punch harder'n the other fellow. Think when you hit."

Tim would seldom leave him in a city. The din of traffic, the leg strain on hard pavement, these were not for his fighter. Shane would chop wood by the hour. It taught him coördination of eye and hand, and made, if possible, his arm muscles stronger.

Shane knew that the hitting power was below the shoulder, that the heavily muscled fighter was at a disadvantage by being "muscle bound," that the great fighter's muscles must be lithe, rippling, tigerish, neither knotted nor bunchy. Heavier muscles were for the wrestler who must pull and maul.

Rory's right hand was used to protect the chin and deal destruction quickly. If his opponent were ready to hit, Shane would not have moved his guard to brush a hornet away.

He could crouch, side-step, weave, bob up and

down, and be equally balanced for a murderous lightning shift in either direction.

To be able to hit equally hard with either hand, his right was strapped to his side. Thus handicapped, he defended himself against two men with his left; later he reversed it, defending himself with the right.

As a "mouth-breather" never had the stamina of one who "breathed through his nose," Shane always kept his lips pressed tight.

Never had a fighter been more carefully coached. A man who mixed caution with daring, Silent Tim would take any chance if the prize were big enough. Though he moved his fighter in and out of small clubs, against men who could not have whipped him except by a miracle, he said many times, "Every dub's dangerous so long as his hands are up—it's the things in the ring that can't happen that do—there's them fighters that play with other men—you wouldn't carry dynamite a half-hour if you could drop it in a minute."

They moved slowly across the country toward New York. Shane had won seven fights.

Joe Mankerlitz tried to bring him into Omaha against Barney McCoy.

"Any time, Joe," said Silent Tim. "We need a ten thousand guarantee—the boy knocked Barney out once, and it wouldn't be a draw any more."

Mankerlitz pleaded with Shane.

"You were tough when you were on top, Joe—who were those gazabos who came into my dressin' room in Cheyenne—I'm the fighter—talk to Tim."

"No grudges, Shane. Those were the little days—you're out of the bushes now."

Silent Tim looked at Shane. "We're after Bangor Lang, the champion."

"But Barney can take him," said Mankerlitz.

"He'll have to do better than he did at Cheyenne." Rory scowled.

McCoy moved forward.

Shane cocked his right.

The managers stepped between them.

"My God"—exclaimed Tim, "you'd fight for nothin' —shame on you!" He pushed Shane backward. "Well, so long, Joe—we gotta keep these roosters apart."

Shane did not speak for several blocks.

"Quit scowlin'," advised Tim, "People'll think you're mad."

After weeks of wire-pulling, Shane was matched with Lang. Unless Lang were knocked out the championship was not involved. If a knockout occurred, Lang was to be given a return match within two months.

"It's a great chance—and we couldn't of got it without Jack Gill. I think Lang's a damn fool myself. If I were him I'd go up against no such man as you for half the house. He can't get over twenty thousand—and you *may* knock him out. I think you're ripe enough to turn the trick. Naturally Jack Gill played you down to get you the chance. But once you're in there, only God can whip you."

Tim's eyes danced.

"Do nothin' the first round—just remember you're fightin' a champion. Somebody's goin' to take Lang soon—and it's goin' to be you—and if you lick him once, you can again—only one man ever got a championship back after he'd been knocked out—Ketchell —may he long sleep sound."

The fight did not end according to Silent Tim's dreams. Shane managed to get a draw—after his jaw was broken.

"It's just one of those things." Silent Tim shook his head in bewilderment. "It can't be helped. The man who wrote 'How to Live to be a Hundred' died at forty-six. He knew how, but he didn't. His jaw got in the way and the Lord called him home."

IX

Shane remained in seclusion for weeks with his bandaged jaw.

Bangor Lang called on him. "It'll be stronger'n ever when it heals," the champion said. "Now don't let it get your goat. You might of won the newspaper decision if it hadn't happened. As it was, you got a draw —and gettin' a draw with me, even without a broken jaw's not done every day."

Shane nodded, smiling.

Lang had majored in chemistry at a university. His father then owned a small drug store. Lang had since acquired a dozen with his ring earnings. His father managed them.

Looking upon pugilism as a business, he was able to veer with all its nefarious winds and become successful. Called "a civilized man" by that peerless authority on things pugilistic, Hot and Cold Daily, he was remarkable in that he used the most ruthless profession in the world as a crutch upon which to lean, and by so doing had made of it an oak under which he gained shelter from future economic storms.

"I started boxin' in the high school gym," he told Shane, "and when I thought I'd be good and knew I'd be a heavyweight, I went in the ring with my eyes on the big dough—we're both lucky, bein' heavy—the heavy guys get the money."

"Sometimes I think it'll be a relief when it's all over. No more chiselers and two-timers—no heartbreak and worry about training. Looking back, I don't know how I ever made it. I don't think I'd ever go through it again. I'd about as soon go to war as to another gymnasium. The fighting's the easiest part of it all—it's the long hours and the waits between fights—and in the early days, it was the desperation for money, or making it hold out till another good match came along. I'd have gone crazy if I hadn't taken up reading. I think I've been through everything. One time I fought a local boy in Bridgeport and every time I got him reeling, the lights would go out. By the time they went on again, he'd be fresh. I guess I hit him so hard it blew the fuses out. Another time I was going on in a main bout and I met one of the boys from the semi being carried into his dressing-room. I got one look at him and knew he was dying. I couldn't get him out of my head all through the fight. It was the hardest I ever had. He died before they got him in the ambulance. His name was Curly Roberts—I'll never forget him."

After many maulings in the ring, Lang was still a handsome man.

"Half the fighters I know are slug-nutty." His tone was low and without anger. "What the devil's the good of a million if you're on your heels? I fought Nealy Rogan four times in as many years. The last two he'd come in the ring just like he was drunk. He'd stagger around for a couple of rounds before he got warmed up. He used to have a rasp in his throat like he'd swallowed files. I've often wondered just what a hard punch does to the brain—it must scatter those cells or weaken them—look at Jerry Wayne—nutty as a walnut tree. He was a dandy in his day—one of the best."

Shane nodded in agreement.

Lang sighed— "Yeap—he was far too good a fellow to hear the bees buzzin' in his bonnet."

Again Shane nodded.

"I'd have quit when I got the first fifty thousand— but I couldn't. It's the fascination of the game, I guess —then there's times a fellow feels he'd be happier nutty —you can't be happy if you see things too clear—some day I'm going to tell all I know about the racket—then I'll jump into the coffin and pull the lid over me and screw it down from the inside."

His heavy hand felt the corrugated ridges of his jaw.

Like Shane, he feared women. Liquor had no place in his life. Neither man considered morals. They were just "bad for fighters."

Shane often wondered, while laid up, just what qualities made a champion. Lang always said, "A champion's the best man—along with other things."

Shane knew that Bangor Lang was a great pugilist. Feinting being a pretense of hitting—to draw an adversary out—Lang was a master at the art. He feinted with his eyes. In his fight with Shane, they darted quickly at a spot he did not wish to strike. Shane was ready to guard the spot, when suddenly Lang's gloves thudded against the opening his eyes had made. After the first round, Shane no longer looked at Lang's eyes.

Lang used every ring trick to his advantage.

When he fought John Atkins, he kept a safe lead at

all times. Atkins, a rushing and vicious fighter, crowded him each round. If he happened to get an advantage, Lang would speed up enough to overcome it. His object was always to keep the decision well in hand. The audience, noting Lang's mastery, demanded that he finish Atkins. Lang merely smiled at the rushing gladiator who was trying desperately to knock him out. At the end of ten rounds, Lang said in his dressing-room, "Well, he has to get along—so I let him stay."

Atkins had asked for no such kindness—he would have granted none himself. He had a world to gain by whipping Lang. The latter had nothing to gain by whipping Atkins too severely. So he could afford to be kind.

So supreme a master was Bangor in the ring that opponents were hard to find. He was accused of "carrying" adversaries so that he might fight them again in some other section of the country. In such a case, it was to his interest to retain the lead and still allow his opponent to make a good showing. In other words, for financial reasons, the master did not dare show his complete mastery. He fought some men a half dozen times, always defeating them by narrow margins. John Atkins was one of these.

Lang was the first to use what later was known as "psychology" in the ring. Among bruisers it was called "getting the other fellow's goat."

While still unknown, he was sent against Jim Murphy, one of the greatest ring sensations that ever lived. Murphy had knocked out the English champion in less than a round. This made him a world's champion.

The match was considered a "set-up" for Murphy, a light workout.

He met Murphy in a restaurant the day of the fight, and said to him quietly, "Be ready tonight, Jim—I'm goin' to tear your head off." He then walked to his own table and ignored Murphy. This was exasperating . . . a cat had not only dared to look at a king— it had brushed its tail in his eyes.

That night Murphy tore at Lang, who sneered, "Come on, you Irish ape—you can't lick a stamp."

Then holding him in a clinch, Lang told Murphy that he had seduced his only sister.

Religious and highly moral, Murphy became insane with rage.

When the gong rang for the second round, the terrible champion rushed at Lang. He was taunted even more about his sister. After each taunt, Lang drove a yellow sledge into Murphy's anatomy, and thus paved the way to oblivion for the champion in the next round.

Murphy later attacked Lang in his dressing-room.

"Take him out of here," sneered Lang, "I don't want to knock him out twice for the same purse."

Murphy shouted, "I'll fight you in the alley."

"Don't be silly—who'll we get to count the house?" sneered Lang.

When his victory was called a fluke, Lang gave Murphy a return match, and knocked him out in two rounds.

Hot and Cold Daily wrote: "Unheralded, unknown, from out of nowhere has come this lad, to become the master of one who was otherwise the master of all the world."

On Lang's first visit, he looked about Shane's room. "What have you got to read?"

Shane shook his head, and motioned to a deck of cards.

"Solitaire, huh—" grunted Lang. "I'll send up some books. I spend a lot of time reading. It's saved my life many a time, drifting over the country. It keeps a fellow from chasin' skirts—besides, you don't have to think when you read."

Shane had never thought about reading.

A messenger arrived with a dozen books.

One was a large history of the ring. Shane looked at the many strange pictures of men who had been champions in the days of James Figg and Jack Broughton.

William Thompson, known as Bendigo, intrigued him most. The first of the illiterate evangelists, and a man of abnormal muscular development, he violated every rule of boxing and became great. He would stand with right hand and foot extended. The first requisite of boxing was the reverse. Shane wondered how he would have fought Bendigo, who defeated the terrible Ben Caunt in ninety-three rounds. One million dollars changed hands on this fight. Shane's eyes opened in amazement.

Caunt, six feet, two and a half inches, was declared the strongest man ever to enter a British prize-ring.

Many old-time bruisers were continually in jail for violating the peace. While Bendigo was in jail for the twenty-eighth time he heard a sermon delivered by the prison chaplain. Upon his release he became the Billy Sunday of his day, and preached salvation in the language of the prize-ring. His points regarding the life everlasting were made with a mighty slapping of hands, large as hams. Multitudes heard him in London.

A memorial was erected to the old bruiser, brother-keeper, and evangelist. It represented a lion sleeping peacefully on a pedestal. Carved below:

"In Memory of William Thompson
(Bendigo)
Who Died
August 23, 1880, Aged 69.
In Life Always Brave, Fighting
Like a Lion,
In Death Like a Lamb, Tranquil
In Zion."

The historian digressed,

"Whether or not pugilists have duller sensibilities than other men has always interested me. Lord Byron boxed frequently with Jackson, a famous bruiser. John Keats was far more pugnacious than most boys. Roosevelt, who had all the qualities of a successful pugilist, except weak eyes, was not a dull witted fellow.

"Heenan, the great American bare-knuckle fighter of the Civil War period, was a man of fine sensibilities. He fought Sayers, the Englishman, for two hours and twenty minutes. The result was a draw. Sayers hit Heenan in the ribs, and the *London Times* correspondent said that the blow sounded 'all over the meadow as if a box had been smashed in.' Thackeray reported the fight for the *Cornhill Magazine*.

"Heenan placed over the grave of his Parisian mistress a marble finger pointing to heaven. Underneath were the words . . . 'Thou knowest.' "

Like a new sponge, Shane's mind soaked in everything. The hotel employees brought him books and magazines. He now passed many hours reading.

Living in a world he had never known, the tranquil days brought dreams.

He thought of the girl he had known on a farm in North Dakota. He started to write her a letter. The words came slowly. The pen scratched. He tore up the letter.

Events of his boyhood stood out clearly. His father, sister, and mother had never seemed so near to him before.

He could see his father sitting in a pine rocking-chair on the little porch, the afternoon sun on him.

Remembering more vividly, he walked about the room.

On Bangor Lang's last visit, he brought a new book. "If you ever feel blue—read this," he said. "It knocked me right out of the ring—here's a blind and deaf girl—nothing stopped her." He handed it to Shane. "She's got a soul like a rose, and more nerve than all of us roughnecks put together."

It was Helen Keller's *Story of My Life*.

"Well, so long, Shane—I've got to be away on an exhibition tour—ten towns in ten nights—but read the book, Old Timer—then read it over—take it from me

it's the best damned thing I've ever read. What a gal!"
He left the room whistling—

> "Just tell them that you saw me,
> And where you saw me last—
> Just tell them I was looking
> well, you know."

The broken-jawed bruiser opened the book and started reading.

Hours passed. He was still lost in the fascinating pages. The girl's struggle, told so simply, caused the tears to come.

Not only was she deaf, but blind. The miracle became greater.

He closed the book with a throbbing heart, and stared at the wall.

"She's seen more than I have," the thought came again and again. He had never been aware of bees and flowers. The blind girl had. The world was a place he had never known.

He opened the book again, then closed it, and rubbed his eyes. Stunned, as if from a blow, he was motionless for some time.

Silent Tim entered, glanced at the title of the book— "What dame are you learnin' about now?" He sighed, "I'll be glad when your jaw heals— No fighter ever got anywhere readin'."

X

When Shane's jaw had healed, Silent Tim Haney said, "Let's go to see Jerry Wayne—you remember him?"

"Yes."

"We keep him where he is—he's too strong for anywhere else. It takes a whole state to watch him." Silent Tim's tone was solemn, as he said, "It was a sad day for a gay man. Jerry was the best welterweight in the world—and when the judge sentenced him to the insane asylum, Jerry says to him, 'I'm still the world's champion—ain't I, Judge?'

"The judge was a puny man. He felt big when he looked at Jerry—like kickin' a lion that's chained.

"He says with a kind of sneer, 'Yes, my dear boy, you are still the champion'—then he slapped his gavel and said, 'Take him away.'

"Jerry tried to shadow box with the handcuffs on him. Then something came to him for a second. He got a flash that he was slug-nutty—and he began to cry"— Silent Tim Haney's eyes narrowed— "I'd of rather fought the Dublin Slasher, old as I am, with bare knuckles, than seen him break.

"His wife looked about the court-room like she didn't want to be there. She was a cheap girl he'd married when he was fightin' semi-windups—he left her near a quarter million and goes away to the nut house."

Silent Tim laughed, "It's a rough world, Shane—as warm as the very devil when the referee's raisin' your hand, and cold as a hangman's heart when he ain't.

"I'll never forget Jerry when he began to come along. He was as nice a-lookin' boy as you'd ever want to see, and of course, like all fighters when he begun to go good, he got himself a diamond and a girl and a tailor-made suit—and a lot of other things that he had no more use for than I have for Joe Slack. But the skirt was something he could of done without—I've never seen a good man yet take one without losin'—and when a fighter takes a broad, it's like takin' the other guy's manager in his corner—the best he can get is chloroform in his lungs—and she'll leave him when he loses. I don't know why it is, but a bad woman hates a fighter —and they're all the poor devils ever get to know. Jerry could of found an excuse for Nero—"

"But they're not all alike, Tim. I know a few that are different," Shane said.

"Where?"

"A little one in Hollywood—I knew her in Cheyenne—another one in North Dakota."

"Huh—they're far enough apart—and even if I knew them I'd stay a bachelor."

Silent Tim rubbed the elk tooth on his watch chain.

"She was all right till Jerry's brains begun to rattle like dry peas in a pod—and then she was no help. She had a little buzzard nose, and bow legs, and she'd talk a lawyer's arm off, with less sense—but poor Jerry— he thought she was the queen of Egypt got lost in the slums."

He looked at his watch. "I've never had any luck with a fighter that got mixed up with a dame—there was the Dublin Slasher—God rest his wild soul—catch 'em young, treat 'em rough, and tell 'em nothin'—the minute you don't, you lose—"

Soon they were in sight of the insane asylum at the edge of the city.

"He was violent for a few days," said the guard. "We had to keep him in a straight-jacket. He thought he was fightin' some fellow for the championship, but he's all right today. I give him a little strap with a buckle on it and told him it was the belt he'd won." The guard smiled. "A fellow has to use his head with these nuts."

Jerry Wayne was seated on a chair, his right elbow on his knee. His body was bent forward as though he awaited the sound of a gong.

He stared blankly at Silent Tim and Shane— "Clear the ring there—clear the ring—I'll git him in this round—" He jumped from the chair and threw blows in every direction. His body contorted as if in pain. He grunted under the impact of imaginary blows.

Dressed in a soft, gray undershirt that showed his muscular shoulders, he stood for a second, beckoning with his left and shouting, "Come on an' fight!" He then blazed away at the empty air.

"God, what a man!" said Silent Tim— "Without a brain in his head he kin lick the king of England—an' the whole English army, three at a time."

Shane watched the insane bruiser intently.

"Do ye think you could lick him?" asked Tim.

He did not answer.

Jerry boxed shadows with bewildering speed.

"Do you remember me, Jerry?" asked Silent Tim as the demented fighter sat on his chair for what he thought was the minute's rest between rounds.

"Sure I remember you. I fought you last night in Paris. You thought you was good till you ducked under a left and bumped into a right—didn't you?"

Silent Tim shook his head.

He stared at Shane, then looked at Tim. "An' that big bozo with you—I'll take him on right now—winner take all. Them big yaps are duck soup for me."

He ran around the room, his elbows at his sides, his fists closed. He stopped suddenly and yelled— "Hey, mister, wait'll my greyhound ketches up—what's all your hurry anyhow?" He walked dejectedly about; then seated himself on a chair, placed his elbows on his knees, his head in his hands, and remained motionless.

The guard said, "He'll sit there all afternoon and never make a move—when night comes I ring a gong."

Shane handed the guard five dollars.

"Thanks—then he comes runnin', an' I say, 'You won agin, Jerry—you're still the world's greatest'—then I take his clothes off an' lay him out on the bed an' let on like I'm rubbin' him down— Purty soon he's asleep."

Fighter and manager walked away in silence.

It was long before Shane asked, "How'd he get that way?"

"More ways than one," replied Tim, "it's not from the beatin's he took—I'd swear to that—it was his damn fool wife. The time I was sick, she was sweet on that big Archie Silvers. Silvers couldn't fight his way out of a paper bag—and she thought he was better'n Jerry —so much do women know of the men who're fools enough to love them. Well, Silvers got too much strychnine and gingerale mixed when he was Jerry's second, while I was away. It went to his brain. That was the beginning. He was nuts on the wife. She's married to Silvers now, anyhow—and even if he couldn't get out of the preliminaries—he's spendin' the money a great main-eventer went crazy to get."

"Jerry was nice to me that time in Butte," said Shane.

"He was nice to everybody," Silent Tim said crisply. "He was too nice to her and Silvers."

With a tone of resignation, Silent Tim said, "But let's forget it—the Lord knows his business— He has as much right to turn a brain over as a cook has an egg."

"I don't think He had anything to do with it." Shane looked ahead, his eyes narrow. "He can't be worried about a lot of goofy fighters."

"Well," Tim demurred, "it wasn't the Lord that slugged him, but He guides us all. If one man goes one way and another a 'tother, I'm sure I'm not the one to lay awake nights to figure it out—I only manage you, and not the world— We've been together quite a while, and you're goin' a long road, my lad." Tim's words rolled easily, "The best man on earth—and there's a million of them—and you're on your way to be the best—think of it, Shaney, my boy."

"Maybe that's what he thought back there." Shane threw his head backward.

"No—he couldn't of thought that—he was only a welterweight—and no man of a hundred and forty-two can lick a great heavyweight, no matter if he's the best welterweight ever born—and that I think Jerry was." Silent Tim paused.

"I knew the night his mind begun to slip. I saw a dead look come in his eye when he fought Harry Sully. He gave Sully a lot of pounds. Sully was lighter then, but still a murderous puncher. He zipped Jerry with a right and left hard enough to glue his teeth together. Jerry said to his wife in the taxi later, 'Hello, Mother, is it rainin' outside?' She didn't have the brains the Lord gives geese, so I said, 'It's a new way he has of teasin', Marie, dear.' For a minute I was a little sad. Jerry was such a gorgeous boy. Such a fine fighter I never saw except the Dublin Slasher and you. He'd move in the ring like he had wings on his shoulders and ball bearin's in his feet."

"What'd you do about him then?" asked Shane.

"There was nothin' I could do," replied Tim, "I couldn't stop him fightin': besides, whatever harm there was, was already done. It was all I could do to keep his body in shape."

"Maybe if he'd of stopped then he'd be all right now," said Shane.

"No, he'd of been on his heels just the same—a slap-happy bum with his wife desertin' him for a preliminary palooka—and now he don't know it. The women who marry fighters, God save my ragged soul, are often crueler than the managers—but anyhow—what's the difference—a little crazy, or crazy all the way—

I'd rather be where Jerry is than hangin' around some fight club havin' the same people who used to cheer me pointin' and sayin'—'There's Jerry Wayne—he used to be a great fighter—you remember. He's cuckoo now.'" Silent Tim was silent a moment. "At least Jerry's not on exhibition," he continued, "There's only two people in the world who go to see him—Wild Joe Ryan, bless his Hebe heart, and myself."

Shane's step had slightly less rubber, as Silent Tim pointed a thumb over his shoulder, "But all the other people in there didn't get slug-nutty fightin'."

"That's right," agreed Shane.

"At least not'n the ring," added Silent Tim.

The manager's voice rose, "But let's forget it. I'm sorry now I took you; for you can't be thinkin' of Jerry Wayne when you go agin' Harry Sully. You gotta keep your head a bobbin' so he don't cut your eye open again—he's got a left jab that's wicked and as quick as the dart of a rattler."

"Don't worry about me," advised Shane.

"I won't—exactly—except, by beatin' Sully now, you'll be in line for Bangor Lang and the championship in a year or two—and if Sully beats you, he'll be. You've already got a draw with Lang, after he broke your jaw."

"Sully'll never beat me," returned Shane, "when Lang couldn't."

"You're right," said Tim. "There's but few men livin' can trade wallops with the Bangor even when their jaws are not broke."

"You've never fought with a broken jaw, have you, Tim?"

"No, my boy—Glory be to the merciful God that's something I missed."

"You'd better thank God—it's like a sharp razor cutting down your neck to your heart every second—there was many a time I saw five Bangor Langs in front of me—I knew I could only hit one—and I didn't dare keep swingin' at the other four, for the referee'd get next and stop the fight—so I'd wait till Bangor got in close and then let him have it—he'd rough my jaw something awful—like gettin' stung with hot needles—but I fooled him." Shane said the last words proudly.

"Bangor's a great fighter—he's every inch a champion," added Silent Tim. "He'll ride for a year or so—and then it'll be you—or Sully." He stopped a second, "Or maybe Torpedo Jones."

"If I don't go slug-nutty like Jerry back there." Shane's head went backward.

"What do you mean—slug-nutty—you're not that kind, Shane, I can tell—you're over the hill now, me boy—no more heart breakin' towns with no money in the house. No more barns to train in, and months without a fight, with no money comin' in. Soon you'll be makin' as much for a week in vaudeville as many a poor slugger gets in a year." He became more earnest. "It's no time to quit now with the race near won."

"I know," Shane agreed.

"You're luckier'n most," continued Silent Tim, "I've got enough money to hire the best, and I made

a lot of it through two boys who're now no more—
Jerry Wayne and the Dublin Slasher—peace to their
wild ashes—for Jerry's dead too—but I played fair with
both of them—there was no nickel they earned they
didn't get. So neither of them can haunt me now."

"Anyhow," said Shane, "nothin' more can happen
to 'em."

"Nothin' more—not even High Mass can disturb
them ever again—and what a God-awful consolation
that is—away from the weepin' and the mock laughter
forever and ever. We didn't ask to be born and we
don't want to die—the boy back there made a million
people forget they were livin' for a minute—and none
of them ever see him now."

"Well, they paid him good money—and they didn't
ask him to be a fighter."

"Why, Shane, you're hardboiled, but you're right—
but let's forget the sad things—if we were as sure of
going to heaven as we are of makin' a few million,
we'd be growin' wings right now."

"You'd be a funny lookin' angel," Shane grinned.

"Maybe so, but I'd be interestin'," added Tim.

XI

For several days Shane trained listlessly. Every movement in the gymnasium brought before him the picture of Jerry Wayne.

Silent Tim was unaware that a fighter could be worried about anything except the outcome of a battle, money, or a woman.

"It'll be all right once the gong rings," he explained. "Sully's a counter-fighter. All you got to do is keep him off balance."

"Yeap—that's all." Shane's words were mocking.

He had seen many punch-drunk fighters. Some had been famous. Others had never left the preliminary class.

The fighter of no ability was as confident as the greatest.

When Tim saw a fighter's leg drag, or his foot scrape the floor, he knew that the inevitable punch-drunk condition was setting in—that nature was collecting for the constant jarring of the brain.

He had seen light "punchers" suddenly become deadly hitters. When their nerves became deadened to pain, they could inflict more.

Several lads he had fought had since gone punch-drunk. Once smiling, carefree, a few years had denuded them of everything but a blank expression.

93

Their heads tilted sideways, a grimace took the place of a smile. Their words were gibberish. The body swayed backward. Deafness came—and often blindness.

They neither blamed nor whimpered. It was "the game." They could always quit. But they never did. Beyond the lure of money, was the fascination that lured them from the valley of boredom, and made it forever impossible to return to humdrum ways again.

"It's the old fire-horse when it hears the bell," explained Silent Tim. "Though its bones rattle, it would race to a fire."

Shane had heard many tales of fighters going "off their nut"—one had charged a street car when the motorman rang the bell—another went crazy in church and jumped up to answer the bell in that awful moment of silence when Christ was supposed to descend upon the altar.

He wondered why Silent Tim had survived, clear-headed, while Jerry Wayne hadn't. He had heard for months about Jerry's fate. It had not impressed him until his visit to the asylum.

Knowing nothing but violence in childhood, he reacted to it with silent but determined belligerency.

A volcano suddenly made quiet, the change bewildered him. Not knowing that in a supreme crisis one is always alone, he wanted desperately to talk to some person.

He had an impulse to explain to Silent Tim, and knew he could not. He remembered what Hot and Cold Daily had said of Harry Sully—"A great fighter

—he's got no imagination." Daily was more sympathetic than the other newspaper writers. Everything was either black or white with them. "If a guy don't want to fight, so what?"

In this mood, Shane fought Harry Sully the second time, the winner to meet Bangor Lang.

Neither fighter looked at the other when called to the center of the ring. Shane looked downward at his gloves. Sully glanced over Shane's shoulder.

"What's wrong with you—what's wrong?" Silent Tim repeated between rounds.

Shane did not speak.

In the third, a glancing blow put him down. "He slipped," a ringsider yelled. Shane was up at once.

At the end of the fight Shane did not even turn to see the referee raise Sully's hand.

The victor, in joy, jumped up and down. His seconds led him to Shane's corner.

Shane sat, his eyes on the canvas floor. He did not look up as Sully touched his shoulder in that gesture of consolation to the loser which the victor does not mean.

To hide his keen disappointment, Silent Tim talked steadily, repeating over and over again, "Next time, next time."

"Sully'll never give him another chance," Wild Joe Ryan said, after they had taken Shane to his room.

"Indeed he will—we'll make him," returned Silent Tim.

"Something's happened to him." Wild Joe Ryan

shook his head. "He fought like a man in a daze."

"He's been fightin' too often," said Silent Tim, "I'll give him a rest."

"He's not burnt out, I hope," said Wild Joe Ryan.

"Nope, it's not that."

"Then what is it?" asked Wild Joe Ryan.

"Nothing," returned Silent Tim, "except Sully's a jinx."

"Maybe he's just a better man," responded Wild Joe Ryan.

"I'll never believe that," snapped Silent Tim, "there's none better alive than Shane Rory."

They looked at each other with unanswered questions in their eyes.

"Is somethin' worryin' him?" asked Wild Joe Ryan.

"No—I guess not—he's a moody boy—something like the Dublin Slasher."

"Wilson couldn't of doped him?"

"Nope—I watched his food and drink—it's just a curtain over his mind—I've seen fighters like that."

Wild Joe Ryan cut in, "He wasn't the lad I saw knock the Nigger out."

"Maybe not—we're not always the same people all the time. Neither was the Nigger in a class with Sully. The higher a fighter climbs, the more accurate the other man's blow, the more strength and cunning to win from them." He sighed. "It was just an 'off night.'"

"He's got to get away from 'off nights' and leave his moods in the dressin' room."

"I know, I know." Silent Tim looked at his comrade with an expression of despair. "It'll be Bangor Lang and Harry Sully now—and my boy can whip 'em both."

"Except—he didn't."

"But he will, you damn fool!" Silent Tim Haney looked scornfully at his friend.

Shane's head rumbled with Sully's punches. He could not sleep.

Thousands of men, riding horses, dashed through the room. All looked like Sully. Pain stabbed above his eyes.

A radio in the next room boomed the result of the fight.

His knees bent. The room circled. The men galloped faster. All now resembled Sully. His sister came quietly toward him, the horses jumping aside as they came near to her.

Sully's eyes were frightful. His hair stood on end, and his face was covered with huge veins of blue and purple.

Shane shook his head fiercely—as though to drive away the effect of a hard blow. His body ached all over. He put his hands to his ears in an effort to relieve the painful throbbing. His eyes became wet.

He threw himself across the bed. Before him waved the wheat fields of North Dakota. He had spent happy months there the year he became a fighter. The priest and the Negro boy and the lad who went away to the penitentiary, and Dilly Dally came before him. That was three or four or five years ago. He tried to think.

He got up, groping. The room whirled around. He fell across the bed.

The back of his head ached from the fury of Sully's "rabbit punches." A stupor came.

Once again he was in North Dakota. The wheat waved. Birds sang above it. Though he could not put it into words, the months there had been the one oasis in the long drudgery of his life. He liked old Peter Lund—and Lyndal. She was something he had never known before. He had left to get her out of his mind.

One of the harvesters had said, "You got a chance there, Buddy—a cat can look at a king—so why can't a road kid look at a gal like that—"

"Stay where you belong," something inside of him had always said, "you're a bum."

He wondered if she were married.

Hand in hand she walked with Dilly Dally. Soon they merged together as one, and kissed his burning lips. Their bodies separated. He could feel their soft hands on his aching forehead. His throat contracted. He tried to encircle both girls. His arms went through them. They were near him again. He could feel the contour of their lovely bodies. The hand of each went through his hair and down his battered face.

Troubled, he dozed.

XII

The telephone rang.

"It's Tim, Shane, sleep well—and don't worry, lad."

A knock came to his door.

"Come in."

A man entered. Shane recognized him.

He had sad eyes, a large pug nose, small teeth, thick lips, and a warm smile. About forty, he had the hard, quick, fat body of one who might have known a rough life in earlier days. A famous writer on sports, his comments were read across the nation. An inmate of a reform school, he ran away. Starting as a boy-of-all-work about a Salt Lake City newspaper, he became a reporter. Unable to write readable English at first, he told his stories or telephoned them. In time, he acquired a racy, vivid way of handling words. At thirty, he had a New York office and his stories syndicated. Never the same for an hour, he was called Hot and Cold Daily.

Short, officious, florid, his hair neither red nor brown, and pompadoured, he moved his heavy body slowly toward Shane and extended a bulgy hand and said, half drunkenly, 'Put it there, Kid—I'm Hot and Cold Daily, Jim Daily to my mother, the greatest sports writer of all degenerate time—they read my stuff in nations yet unborn. I gave you a break tonight.

I saw something in your eyes when you were in that ring, Shaney, my boy. I said to myself, 'I'm goin' to talk to that kid and keep his heart from breakin'.' Then I met a lot of other reporters and I got a snoot full—but the will is strong, my boy, and when it was all over, it said to me, 'Go and see Shane Rory—he's too good a young stallion to be hamstrung like he is.'" He pulled a hip-shaped silver flask from his pocket—"Napoleon brandy—Shaney—it's all I drink on a fight manager. Al Wilson gave it to me—but I saw that hurt look in your eyes, Kid, and I said to myself— 'Ah—the furies are getting him—.'"

He touched Shane's arm, "There was mercy in your heart, Roaring Shane Rory—you're the deadliest ring killer in the world today when you want to be. Sully fought—and Sully won all right—won by what Bismarck—or Jim Jeffries—would call one of the imponderables. He shouldn't have won, but he did. And listen, Shane—mercy might drip like the gentle rain from heaven and the quality of it may not be strained—but it has no place in the prize-ring. You could have stopped him in the fifth when he started to crumple—you could have stopped a freight train with your fists—that was a great round—the greatest ever—you were a human bolt of lightning—and your blows were thunder."

Hot and Cold Daily looked at Shane, whose head was buried in his hands, his elbows on his knees.

"Don't sit there like a statue of 'The Thinker,' Kid—it'll all pass." He swigged at his flask again and chanted,

" 'Let it be forgotten, as a flower is forgotten,

Forgotten as a fire that once was singing gold,
Let it be forgotten forever and ever,
Time is a kind friend, he will make us old.' "

He whirled around, "Forget it, Shane—I put you on
the grease a little in my story—but you'll understand—
we writers have to live. I don't know why—but I made
you a great guy, Shane—in spite of that—you're tops
with me. I think you're a hell of a swell guy. You're
like all us fellows who crawl through somehow—your
job's to fight, and mine's to write the truth sometimes—
as I see it. Many a guy paid enough to feed a family
for a week to see you battle tonight—and you owed it
to yourself to give your best—here's something I wrote,
the way I saw it:

" 'What brought about that crumpling was a whizzing right, in the form of a hook. It nailed Sully, a little
high on the jaw. It was not quite on the button. If it
had been, Sully would be out yet. His knees buckled.
He began to go down. Rory's right was only twelve
inches back. It shoved in again like a piston rod, and
caught Sully the same way. It knocked his jaw to one
side. He began to collapse. Sully, who never gave
mercy to any man, who would knock his own mother
out of the ring if you put her in there with him, Sully
appealed with his eyes to Roaring Rory not to hit him
again. And Roaring Rory for a moment had mercy—
and Sully went down with his wild and merciful antagonist standing over him, ready to deliver blows that
would have paralyzed a bull. *And he did not deliver
them.*

" 'Those who saw that round can never forget. I

picture to you Sully, a man with shoulders three feet wide, and muscles like a rhinoceros, crumpling before the fury of Roaring Shane Rory. All credit to Rory, and pity for his mercy. No man but Sully of the powerful heart could have risen from the canvas.

" 'It was a great brawl. You could hear the swish of their fists a dozen rows from the ring.

" 'A condor flying was no more graceful than Roaring Rory. What will become of him? Ask me something with a happy ending—' "

Shane stood erect.

"Now tell me, Shane—what happened?"

"I don't know," answered Shane, "I couldn't get going. I'd say to my body— 'Come on now, go in and slug till his ears fall off,' but I couldn't get going. My body's always been like a pal to me. It went back on me with Sully. He got so he looked like Jerry Wayne."

Hot and Cold Daily's eyes slanted upward at the handsome, chisel-jawed bruiser.

"Tell me, Shane—have you been doin' much thinkin' lately? You know a fighter's like a newspaperman—he shouldn't think—pimps of the emotions, that's what I call us fellows. Now you've got everything—but for God's sake don't develop brains. That's what kills people. Never let 'em tell you different. This world was made for the boobs, for the guy who can never get enough dough to pay for a lousy radio, who just gets his furniture half paid for when his oldest girl graduates and that sets him back half a grand.

"So don't develop brains—let them all go crazy trying to find the answer. You've got it when you don't try to find it. It's all a shadow on a cloudy day—two cents in a bum's pocket when a loaf of bread is seven. For a second you weren't a fighter . . . and Sully was.

"Now, quit worryin', Shane—or you'll turn out to be one of us, and know everything not worth knowing. A young fighter might give you a dime when you're through; but a kid on a newspaper won't have one to give you.

"Don't lie to yourself, Shane, but to everybody else —for when life itself is a lie one more or less won't matter before you ride the white horse of eternity into the desert. But tell yourself the truth.

"It's all a dish of old berries, Shane. Even freedom's another jail, and even the hangman's under sentence of death, thank God.

"Nothing ever changes and nothing ever will—the boob gets socked like a preliminary fighter, and he hasn't got brains enough to know that it's all a goose-step to the grave; so he grabs at one cock-eyed illusion after another to keep his damn fool heart from breaking. You show me a fool without an illusion, and I'll show you a philosopher.

"When I was a kid in the reform school, we used to sing—

> " 'Where was Moses when
> the lights went out?
> Sitting in the window with
> his shirt tail out—'

"Well, we're all sitting in the window, Shane—and don't get too many brains."

Shane watched the dawn streak in.

Hot and Cold Daily reached for the phone. "Send a quart of brandy to 844." He turned to Shane. "I've got to get some sleep tonight—I mean today."

He turned to leave, saying,

"Put it all behind you, Kid— Even Napoleon got his —he gave a lot out and squawked like a hurt duck when they handed it back to him. See you later."

Shane did not move.

Hot and Cold Daily returned to him. "Brace up, Kid. We're both Irish—and we have traditions." He laughed. "A kindlier race never tore a man to bits— Good night."

XIII

The door closed without noise. Shane watched it for a moment; then opened it again.

His head was light. Pain darted above his eyes.

The echo of his footsteps could be heard in the still silent street. Why had he never thought of returning to the farm in North Dakota? The entire city became a swiftly revolving wheel.

He walked for blocks. A dizziness came. He stumbled into a small hotel. Still early morning, the lobby was empty except for a patriarchal old man, whose white beard was so heavy it seemed to pull his scrawny shoulders downward. His skin was sallow in the broadening light. His nose was long and thin, his mouth woe-begone.

Though he could have been no more surprised had an eagle flown into the dingy office, his alert eyes made no sign.

"Can I do something?" the old man asked.

"Yes, put me to bed—I'm sick."

The old man led him down a hallway to a room on the first floor.

"You'll be all right here," he said, "I'll come back later." He knew who Shane was. He read all the newspapers thrown about the lobby.

Shane fell into bed. The old man covered him.

Locking the door, he went slowly down the hall-way. Putting the key to the room in his pocket, he took a faded piece of pasteboard, with a string attached, and bearing the words, "DO NOT DISTURB." He returned and hung it over the doorknob.

Through his old head ran all the wisdom acquired in the sewers of life. He knew that Shane was not drunk—that he must have been hurt in the ring. If he were not heard from in time, something might be in the newspapers. He would take no chances.

He returned to the room. Shane was in a deep sleep.

He moved about, saying as a blind, "Let me help you take off your clothes."

The fighter breathed heavily, without response. His thin gold watch had fallen to the floor. The old man fingered it; then placed it on the dilapidated dresser. To pawn it would be a give-away.

"Here's your watch," he kept saying, "It fell on the floor."

He touched Shane's trouser pocket. It bulged. Lightly and greedily his ancient fingers went into it. A stack of paper money, folded carelessly, came out.

Hastily the old man counted some bills of smaller denomination and put them back in Shane's pocket, along with the watch. "Anyone robbin' him would take his watch," he thought.

His hand went into Shane's inside coat pocket and removed a soft leather billfold. It contained many fifty and hundred dollar bills. He started to leave four bills. His avarice predominated. He left two fifty dollar bills and replaced the folder.

Putting the key in the lock on the inside of the room, he left.

The cellar had a loose stone in the foundation. Avidly the old man counted the money—nearly two thousand dollars. He put the stone in place, and returned to the desk.

Shane regained consciousness on the morning of the next day.

He went to the dingy lobby and gazed for a few moments into the street; then started to open the door.

"Are you leaving?" the old man asked.

"Yes."

"Two dollars, please."

Shane paid the money, and walked without sense of direction about the city, and stopped in a saloon, where he ordered several strong drinks and again wandered aimlessly about the city.

When Silent Tim learned that Shane had gone, he shook his head dolefully. "I've never seen a great fighter yet that wasn't wild as the wind." Nonplused, he looked around the lobby, and seated himself in a large leather chair.

"I wonder where he'll show up next—he's wild as the wind—the poor boy—wild as the wind." He rubbed his eyes with a knuckle-cracked hand. "He's still a better man than Sully— Him and Jerry Wayne and the Dublin Slasher," he said, "aces to draw from," he sighed, "and that black Torpedo Jones—if he only was white." A smile crossed his weather-beaten face. He pictured Shane Rory and Torpedo Jones in the ring.

"It's seldom that two such great men get in the ring

at their peak together. It may be just as well. They'd shake the world with their punches."

He mused for a moment, "I'll say nothing to the papers."

His eyes were dim.

"I'm catchin' cold—damn it!"

XIV

A girl looked at him as he staggered into a night club.

"Good-looking, isn't he?" she asked the man with her.

He turned. "Yes, if you like 'em rough."

She went to Shane's table, and said, "Gee, I've always wanted to meet you— I knew you when I was a little kid."

"That so? Who's the fellow with you?"

"Just a friend," she answered.

"He's liable to come over and beat up on me." He laughed deliriously.

The girl smiled. "I'd like to see anybody *beat up on you.*"

He called a waiter. "Give us a drink."

She shook her head. "I'm not drinkin' on you— I've got a live one over there." She nodded.

"You wouldn't kid me, would you?" Shane reached for the drink smiling.

"I'm not the kidding kind," she answered. "I could of cried when you lost. Hot and Cold Daily told me something was wrong."

Shane looked at her earnestly.

"I'm not what you think." Her tone was whimsical and mocking. She nodded toward her companion. "I keep men like him under control."

Shane looked at his glass.

"Are you sure you don't need me?" she asked.

"Not me, Kid."

"I work here. Don't get me wrong."

"You're all alike."

"Your manager's been telling you things—I've heard about him."

"Where?"

"Everywhere—he's better know than the Brooklyn Bridge."

"And just as safe," returned Shane.

"And as blind—a bridge can't tell sick people from well—it carries them all the same."

His eyes became glazed.

She called a waiter.

"Get a cab. He's sick."

She returned to her companion. "See you later." To the waiter, "Look after him."

She entered the cab with Shane. "Imperial—Central Park West."

Shane was mumbling, "Come on, stumble bum—it's the last round—let's throw some leather—you couldn't knock me out if you had the moon in your glove—eh— Tim—see that little girl over there—that's Lyndal Lund —she lives in Grainville, that's North Dakota—you know her—ho! ho! ho!—the glory road—the glory road— 'I'se goin' to push leather down the glory road.' "

"Drive through the park a while," the girl said, while Shane continued to mumble.

The girl was pensive. The past hurried by.

She had heard of him all her life. When his name began to creep into the newspapers, she sent a letter to him in care of a Chicago sports editor. "Tell me," she wrote, "if you're my Shane Rory." She mentioned what her father had told about him. The letter was never answered.

His name became fixed in her mind. If his fight were too unimportant to warrant a paragraph in a New York newspaper, she turned to the section—"Fights Last Night." She often found Shane Rory's name—and after it, "Won" or "draw"—and the number of rounds. It was more than the career of a fighter to her. It made the young road of her days glow as if the morning sun were upon it. He came out of the same neighborhood.

He was always "the little Rory kid" to her father. He would read of him and say, "The boy has nerve— his father was a slash of a man. It's the great blood in his veins—the Roarin' Shane Rory—eh—that fellow Daily can name them—his father could roar a cyclone down."

Shane again mumbled,

> " 'Oh the glory road, the glory road—
>   I'm goin' to push leather
>   down the glory road.' "

Her father had speculated on Shane's chances with Bangor Lang—and never learned the result.

The lights slanted across Shane as the cab rolled along. She had never seen such strength. His immense shoulders bulged in the well tailored coat.

She recalled his fight with Sully. What a great man Sully must be—to get a decision over him.

He moved quickly. "Where are we?"

"In Central Park." In sudden fear that he might want to leave, she talked rapidly, "I'm taking you with me—my dad knew yours—you'll trust me, won't you —Daddy was a cop till he got killed—and here we are— their two kids trying to find out what it's all about— life's funny, huh—nutty as a wedding cake, and all gummed up with a lot of sticky things. It was the day you fought Bangor Lang that Daddy was killed. I wanted to come to you then and introduce myself, but I was a little jittery—it's heaven to love someone; but it's hell when he slips away—it leaves an empty place the whole earth can't fill."

Shane pulled the fingers of his hand. The knuckles cracked like bullets.

He looked around the cab.

The girl talked swiftly.

"Daddy told me all about you as a kid—when I saw your picture several days ago I said to myself, 'Gee, I'd like to know him again—your hair's like mine, huh?'"

Shane remained quiet. The hard ridge of his jaw was low on his chest.

The slender hand of the girl touched his face.

"Want some money?" he asked.

"No—damn your money—I'm not working tonight. . . . Let me help you—I mean it—I can still hear my dad sayin'—'If that broke little bastard makes good, there's a chance in the world for everybody,' and I believed him. I'm your pal—you can't go around this way. Ask Hot and Cold Daily about me."

Her green gown clung to her slender body. Sheer stockings on lovely legs, satin slippers, auburn hair in waves, she was a vivid contrast to Shane.

"You're purty," he said in a half-conscious drawl.

"Keep the change," she laughed, "So you think I'm a girl of the night—and me in a thirty dollar seat to see you fight. I'm an entertainer, Shane—Berniece Burue—fancy name for Mary Cassidy." She put her card in his upper coat pocket, "If you get lost, strayed, or stolen, ask for me. I sing silly songs and play a violin—men play with me—give me tips on the stock market, and when they don't get to first base they quit the game. . . . Well, here we are."

"I'd rather not go in," he said.

"Come on—it's all right."

She stood at the cab door.

He got out, looked up and down the fashionable street, said, "So long," quickly, and vanished into Central Park.

She watched him for a second; then handing the driver money, she went into the elevator.

Going to the telephone, "This is Berniece Burue—Do me a favor Hoten Cold?"

"Sure thing, Berniece—"

"Shane Rory just left me. I'm here at the Imperial—he went over into the park—he's slightly—you know—maybe you can call some of the cops—confidential—and find him—don't say anything—please—"

"I won't—thanks, Berniece—he must be slug-nutty to leave you. So long."

She gazed over the wilderness below. A thick haze

hung over the park. Lights gleamed dimly through the trees.

"Well, that's that," she said, "What a man—and my people—his dad and mine."

XV

Completely conscious in the railroad station at South Bend, Indiana, he tried to recall what had happened. Vaguely the fight with Sully returned to him.

He bathed his eyes in cold water, and looked at himself in the mirror. His cheeks were sunken. He felt for his watch. It was gone.

He found a crumpled card in his pocket.

He remembered the girl and his leaving the cab.

A Negro attendant applied a whiskbroom to his clothes. Shane fumbled in his pocket. "Here, Mate." He flipped a twenty-five cent piece.

"I doan guess you got no moah." The Negro advanced with the quarter.

"That's all right," remarked Shane. "I've got a few dollars."

"No, you ain't—you's all in, down an' out. I can tell."

"Who, me?" Shane smiled slowly.

"Yes suh— I let's you sleep heah all night— Fly cop he come in an' looks at yuh an' I says you's my frien' so he goes on out an' you keeps talkin' 'bout a fahm in No'th Dakota an' fightin' somebody."

He put the quarter in Shane's hand. Shane tried to hand it back. The Negro repeated, "No suh, no suh," and ambled away.

He found his way to the Midland Labor Agency in Chicago.

Men jostled each other in a large room on West Madison Street. Some had blankets tied to sticks slung across their backs. They were the familiar "bindle stiffs" or men who carried bundles in a wandering world. Old "jungle buzzards," the parasites of tramps, loitered about in the throng—the poor begging of the poor.

Written in chalk on a huge blackboard were the words:

"400 MEN WANTED FOR NORTH DAKOTA—GRAINSVILLE AND ADJACENT POINTS—CHARGES $2.00—FULL SHIPMENT MUST BE HAD IMMEDIATELY—"

A "man-catcher" touched Shane's arm. "You look like you could do a day's work. Go get a valise to show good faith."

When he returned, the man said, "All right—two dollars, please—over to one side—North Dakota—Rolling River Farm—first gang—Red River Valley next—get in line there, boys."

They were marched to the depot, and put in a once gaudy but now old-fashioned passenger car.

On Sunday morning they were in the Red River Valley of North Dakota.

Wonder at what had happened since he left brought surcease from more hectic memories.

He gazed out of the dusty window as the train rumbled through small, flat towns. Combining a red railroad station, a listless flagman at a crossing, a short main street, a cattle pen, and a tall grain elevator, they were as much alike as knots in a string he remembered. Small school buildings and fantastic frame houses, with lightning rods gleaming above turrets and cupolas, were scattered over the level land.

From Grainsville, they were taken to the four thousand acre Rolling River Farm.

A graveled road went directly to the house. Of faded brick, with green shutters, it was a huge, sixteen-room box, half hidden by trees. It had been built by a farmer for whom Peter Lund, the present owner, had worked as a hired hand.

Red buildings, with slate roofs, and larger than his house, were all about. An office, built of logs, was at the edge of his barnyard, two hundred feet from the house. A large map of the world and a larger one of the United States was on the wall. Magazines and books were everywhere in the office.

A Danish peasant, and silent as falling snow, Lund left his land but seldom.

He had married the girl on the next farm. A country school teacher, she taught him to read and write.

Slow of speech and movement, and sturdy and wind-beaten as the maples about the house, he was very tall. Though seventy, he was the equal in strength of any man who worked for him. His shoulders were bent with labor. He was, in his every action, the master of four thousand acres—and himself.

The same migratory laborers had come to his farm for years. He paid them every week, and allowed them to draw money each day for anything needed.

He would listen to their tales with a slight glint of humor.

All on the large farm, including his wife, called him "the Boss." Lyndal, his daughter, called him "Daddy Denmark." She now joined him. Two Great Danes followed. He had given them to her years ago when Shane was on the farm. She called them Norway and Sweden.

Lund watched the caravan coming from the door of his office. There was a quizzical expression about his eyes as if he were wondering for a moment about these mysterious men who came and went indifferently as the seasons, without regret, without hope, and as seemingly carefree as the wind across his fields.

Shane was the last of the group. Lyndal watched them all, smiling, until he came.

Startled, her eyes met his. How powerful he had grown.

"It's nice to see you again, Shane."

"I'm glad to be back—it's like home," he replied bashfully, in a half daze, and moved away.

Now above six feet, with heavy drooping shoulders, his jaws were sharp and protruding.

Peter Lund turned to his daughter, as a rift of wind blew a wisp of brown hair, the color of her eyes. Her figure was curved and slender, her lips full and red; her heart beating fast, her eyes followed him.

"He's back again, eh, daughter?"

"Yes, Daddy—I'm glad."

"A fine-looking fellow like that driftin' around like a cloud." Her father's eyes went upward.

"It's what I'd do if I were a man."

"Be glad you're not a man," he said, as, outwardly calm, she went to the house.

She had often wondered what had become of him.

He had stayed from the beginning of the harvest until she had gone to college. A letter she had written to him had been returned by her mother with the news that he had left suddenly. She was so used to him that it did not seem possible he would leave as suddenly as he came.

He was everywhere on the farm. If someone were needed to go on an errand to Grainsville, Shane went. She often went along. Those were happy hours. She was proud of his reverence for her.

She remembered him saying, "I'm a road kid—some morning I'll be gone."

She did not dare show concern.

With Shane and her father, she felt secure. She thought how much alike they were.

The years had given her time to compare. His silence had been more to her than the talk of other boys. He had asked her questions about everything. She had caressed him slightly in leaving for college.

She gazed out of the window across the waving fields. In the distance was the red brick schoolhouse she had attended as a child.

Pupils and teachers returned to her. Irvin Rogers had taught her two seasons. He had lived at her house. She would have married him had "the boy" not come to the farm. Unconsciously he had filled her with unrest, uncertainty. She had been more contented with "the boy."

He stood alone now, near the windmill.

She went to him.

A stillness that comes now and then in the wheat country followed. Everything stopped moving at once. Horses stood, their heads down, their eyes half closed. Hens did not cackle. Roosters did not crow. Over the ground passed a long wave of shadow.

"Isn't it wonderful?" She looked at the young giant before her.

"Yes—it is," Shane replied.

"Where have you been so long?"

"Every place," was the answer.

"Didn't you ever think of us here? We wondered about you."

She wore a form-fitting brown sweater, a bright yellow scarf, and white flannel skirt.

"You look beautiful."

"Thank you—but my question."

"Yes, a lot of times. I started a letter to you once."

Pleased, "Did you? Why didn't you finish it. I'd have loved it."

"I don't know," at a loss for words. "You're growing up."

"So are you." She smiled, looking up at him.

"How's your grandmother?" he asked.

"Didn't you know? How could you? She died a few months after you left."

Lyndal's grandmother was a Sioux Indian. She died

on a windy January morning, her clay pipe clutched in her hand. The funeral stretched for a mile over the frozen ground. Lyndal was more drawn to the old lady than to her own mother. She had inherited a slender body, a lithe, graceful walk, and a love of Indian lore from her grandmother. Mrs. Lund had put aside all things Indian in girlhood.

The stern, unyielding old woman, and her equally determined father had influenced Lyndal's life. For hours she would form a trinity of silence with them. As close to them as the soil, she loved the ripple of wheat, the patter of rain, and the primitive sweep that made up their lives.

Her mother was never quite of the group.

As Peter's lands and money grew, his wife became more and more fastidious. She abhorred the sweating bodies of the harvesters and their salt-streaked clothing. A slight, dark woman, she was a contrast to her immense husband.

The mood of nature lifted. Everything stirred.

The farm was more vivid in color. Birds flew with more graceful motion through the bright, blue weather.

Fleecy white clouds sailed before the sun and dappled the ground with shadow.

Her mother called.

Lyndal went to her.

"Well, he's back," she said.

"Yes," returned Lyndal. "He's changed, hasn't he?"

"And not for the better, I'm afraid," returned her

mother. She glanced at Lyndal. "He was such a nice-looking boy—he's harder now."

"He's stronger and bigger—more of a man," said Lyndal.

XVI

Work began at dawn. The sun was soon shining, yellow and hot as a furnace blaze through the whirling dust of the cloudless sky. Hitched to a large machine, twelve horses plodded slowly through the clank and roar of the field.

The grain fell in wide sheets, on a long apron that carried it into a machine. The straw was dropped on the ground, the grain into sacks from a tube at the side.

Because of his strength, Shane was put to loading the heavy sacks of wheat. He tossed them into the waiting wagons that hauled them from the field. It was the hardest work of the harvest.

Tireless and cheerful, the men worked early and late. There would be "get-togethers" as Peter Lund called them, after supper. Knowing the strain of labor, he liked to see the men relax—when sixteen hours of the day had gone. If he was a driver of men, nature drove him. His thousands of acres ripened quickly.

There was a respite of twenty minutes in mid-afternoon. Lyndal took lunch to the men. Friendly to all, she did not forget that her father had once been a hired man.

He was well known in the Red River Valley.

The prey of nature for years, he had seen hot winds

burn his fields in an hour—the labor and hope of months. He accepted ill or good fortune without change of expression. His eyes would follow a bobolink darting up and down with the undulating waves of his yellow fields with the same satisfaction that he gazed at a copper sun that betokened good weather. The chinch bug, the Hessian fly, the locust of old, he fought all in turn with the same determined calm. A fatalist, he fretted neither against nature nor events.

Each spring he would walk for miles across his fields to discover where the snowdrifts of winter had washed away his wheat. Later, he would watch the green coloring turn to a lighter shade and then to yellow until his wheat was ready for the harvest.

One morning, after a rain, the wheat was too wet to handle. A whirring noise was heard above the barnyard.

"Sounds like locusts," an old laborer said to Shane. "They used to be a lot of 'em around. I'll never forget my first year here. They came like so many clouds—the sun shining on their wings so they looked like a million specks of glass moving. The wheat was just getting ripe. There was nothing the boss could do but let them come. The sun was about two hours up in the sky. The boss watched them settle down—and I watched him. I thought I'd rather be a bum than have what was in his heart when he saw another swarm coming up in front of the sun and making it dark as a horse's mouth.

"The boss looked at them, hoping they wouldn't light on his fields—nor any other fields nearby—for whatever else you can say about the old man, he's not mean. They flew above the farm for three days. There were whole hours when you couldn't see the sun. Old Peter knew if they ever lit, they'd clean his fields like a starving man would a platter of meat. They traveled in long waves like the pictures of a comet's tail. A bunch of them took a notion to light on old Peter's far field the third day. He took it standing up. His little girl looked up at him and said, 'Brave Daddy.' I can see her yet—she was a cute little shaver. He held her close against his right leg, his big paw covering her whole right shoulder—and he never said a word. I've never quit liking him since that day. It was a hundred acre field—they might eat up his farm and they might leave in an hour—you could see them going down in front of the sun, bent like rainbows, their wings all aglisten. Some of the women started beating a tin tub to scare them away. They might just as well have whistled 'Yankee Doodle' for all the good it did—

"'Don't play any music for them—they can eat without that,' the boss said.

"We all sat around in the yard and listened to the whirring of locust wings until the sun went down. The next morning early, we rushed down to the field. There was a billion of them up in the sky already flying like a lot of wild geese. They'd stripped that field like a fire'd gone over it. It was bare as a cow's nose. There was an old wagon at the edge of the field that had hickory shafts. They cut a furrow in them like you would with a corn knife. All of a sudden, those on the ground shot up and bunched with the others. We could hear their wings droning like electric fans going at high speed. They didn't light for over thirty miles, and then they ate up a poor devil's farm along the Red River.

"The boss' wife had prayers said in church the next Sunday, thanking God for steering the locusts away.

"The boss said, 'I wonder why He steered 'em to Lars Anderson's farm?'"

Two laborers sparred good naturedly.

"I wonder how the fight came out," the teller of the tale said.

"I don't know," answered another, "Who's fightin'?"

"Bangor Lang and Harry Sully."

"Funny how people like fights," the man who told of the locusts looked at Shane. "I used to work on a ship that hit Alaska every ten months. It was after Jeffries fought Johnson. We were going about a half mile from shore when an old trader came out in a whale boat with some Eskimos in it. He begun to hail us, and we thought maybe he thought we were his supply ship that brought him mail and stuff once a year. We slowed down until he got within yelling distance. Then he put his hands to his mouth and yelled, 'Who won the fight?'

"'What fight?' we all yelled at once.

"'Jeffries and Johnson,' he yelled back.

"'Jack Johnson,' we all shouted.

"He sat down in the boat and hung his head. Soon

he motioned the Eskimos to row him back to shore. It must have been ten months after the fight."

The tale ended, a pause followed.

"Neither of them could lick Harry Sully," was a laborer's comment.

Shane might have been a giant statue with shoulders wide as a granary door. Soon his powerful hand opened and closed.

He did not speak.

XVII

A Sunday newspaper with Hot and Cold Daily's syndicated account of the heavyweight championship fight between Bangor Lang and Harry Sully came to Rolling River Farm.

Sully had knocked Lang out.

"For twelve rounds," Shane read, "the fight was a great one, a fight that sent tingles up your spine and kept you sitting on the edge of your chair, eyes glued to the ring. It was a bitter, punching battle, with Sully forcing the going and punishing Lang but with the latter lashing out with his right continuously. Sully walked right into him as the brawl started, smashing his right to the body. At long range he jabbed and hooked lefts to Lang's head. And when the end came, the lion-hearted Lang slumped to the canvas. When ten was counted, his seconds carried him to his corner.

"He was limp as a rag. Once seated on his stool, he immediately slid off, and then, in a sort of spasm, began kicking and squirming until his befuddled handlers stretched him out on the ring floor and the boxing commission's physician went to work on him. He remained there for a half hour while the thousands who attended the fight gathered about the ring and craned their necks to watch him and the restorative measures being employed to bring him around. Finally he was lugged off to his dressing-room, where several doctors worked over him for another hour before he was taken from the building."

The lure of the ring returned.

Lang was a better man than most, a real sport.

After Shane's bad luck in their fight, he remembered Lang had said, "I'm sorry, Shane. If I can help, let me know—it's all in the racket. Even if you win—you lose." And now Bangor had lost.

Bangor knew when to laugh. The night he knocked Cotton Socks Lubin out, a drunken man entered Lubin's room by mistake. The defeated fighter was resting beneath many towels.

"Bangor, my lad—I'm glad you knocked hell outta that Hebe."

Lubin jumped from the table and chased him from the room.

Shane smiled in memory.

A voice yelled, "Hey, you fellows—they want the paper up at the house!"

A laborer hurried away with it.

"It was a dinger of a fight," he said, handing the paper to Lyndal. She took it to her room.

She read the description and turned the page. Before her was a picture of Roaring Shane Rory. Beneath it were the words, "Where now is the mighty Shane Rory?"

Never before had anything touched her so completely. Shane Rory, "the boy," was a prize-fighter.

Why had he given up the ring?

She crossed the yard to the living quarters of the men and called, "Shane!"

She went with him to her father.

"We're going to Grainsville—you don't mind, do you, Daddy Denmark?"

"Not at all."

A short distance down the road, she said, "I saw your picture in the paper this morning. . . . So you're a prize-fighter?"

"Yes."

Her manner was gentle.

He became silent.

"Why did you leave the ring?"

"I had to." He hesitated— "I was afraid—"

"Afraid—"

"Of going slug-nutty—crazy."

She stopped the car in the shadow of a grove; then touched his powerful hand. "Tell me, Shane,—what's wrong?"

"Nothing—I'm broke inside."

"What caused it?"

"Everything."

"You can talk to me—" —she looked in his eyes— "and trust me. I see so much in you—besides—"

He began slowly, "Well, I went to see Jerry Wayne, a great fighter, in the insane asylum. I couldn't get him out of my head—then I fought Sully, who's now champion, and lost— I remember wantin' to come here. Then I passed out and still remembered when I came to—that's how I happened to get here. Once before, when I had my jaw broke, I started to write you a letter, but I gave it up— Something happened to me, anyhow, after I'd seen Jerry Wayne at the asylum.

That made everything sharper—and brought a lot of things back that happened when I was a kid."

"Didn't you have a home—or a father and mother, like other boys?" she asked.

It was several minutes before he answered.

"I did for a little while—then things happened fast. My dad was laid up for six months one time—and we didn't have any money. My sister was five years older'n me—we stayed home with him, and my mother went to work at night, scrubbin' the floors of a big office building. One night on her way home, she was pushed off a moving street car. She never came to, and died that morning. The conductor said the man who pushed her off was drunk; anyhow, he got away."

Lyndal gripped the wheel.

"Well, that was that." He made an effort to lighten his tone. "People were kind—I've got to say that for 'em. The street car company gave us a hundred dollars. I can remember more'n anything going around among a lot of coffins with my sister—and remember her payin' eight dollars for one— Sis would cry at night with me —but never in the daytime when anyone was watchin'.

"The shock did something to Dad. He braced right up. He was a stone-mason when he worked; so he got a job on the Panama Canal and went there. He left us behind with some neighbors. We were everybody's kids, and soon we were nobody's.

"I'll never forget how happy we were when my sister got a letter from him sayin' he was comin' home. He sent her fifty dollars to pay on furniture. So she got a little place all fixed up—and the day the boat came in we were both awake before daylight. I've never seen anything like it comin' in— We watched all the people get off. Then the captain came up to tell us as easy as he could that our father had died and was buried at sea."

Lyndal gasped slightly.

"Well, there we were in a spot. The furniture company was decent and gave us back the fifty—and the woman didn't charge anything for the apartment. I don't like to tell everything that happened. Things are never with kids like they are in story books.

"My sister was never very strong. She used to tell me I was like my father—he could bend a dime with his fingers. They wanted him to be a fighter when he was young—but he wouldn't. Mother was Norwegian. I can remember hearin' her cough in the morning after she'd come home from work. We just lived like sparrows. I got fourteen dollars one week settin' up pins in a bowlin' alley—a lot of teams were playin'—I was about thirteen then. I gave it nearly all to Sis, and she turned around and bought me a lot of things. She was like that. She was everybody's drudge—all she ever did was work—the one thing I most remember was her waitin' on Dad. She had to be doin' somethin' for people or she wasn't happy. She died quick of gallopin' consumption—and there I was again."

He turned to Lyndal. "I had to take it. It's funny— I don't know why—nobody ever thinks a boy has any troubles—but he has—plenty. There was a man with a bowlin' team that liked me. He had a place in Cleveland. I took a freight train there. I could tell you a lot about that—but I won't—pretty soon I was runnin' errands for a lot of fighters around a gymnasium.

"I learned to box hangin' around there. I slept in the poolroom, on one of the tables, next to the bowlin' alley—and the first thing you know, I was a fighter. The thing I can't figure out is why I didn't start fightin' sooner—I don't remember ever learnin' to box like most kids—"

Lyndal clasped his hand. "I can't tell you how much I admire you. Just to survive and be so decent after all that is a great deal."

He did not move.

"Remember," she said, "how we caught the Canadian wild goose so exhausted in the barnyard that summer—and how it stayed for a week until it was strong again—then one morning we watched it fly toward the sun, and circle to the west—honking good-bye forever." She moved closer to him. "That was the way you left."

She yielded to his embrace.

"I'm sorry," he said, trembling.

"You needn't be."

The doleful whistling of the Fargo Express could be heard across the fields.

"There's everything here," she said. "I own my grandmother's farm—we can be happy watching things grow." She listened for a moment to the birds in the grove. "I love it here—the land is so restful— each spring is a new beginning—and with you here— it's too wonderful."

In her heart was unutterable longing.

When they reached home, she kissed him impulsively.

She remained long in his arms. All the rough years of his life were worth this moment. The enormous hands that had battered so many men now held her against him. He tried to say something. The words choked in his throat. Several minutes passed. She made an effort to move away. His tremendous shoulders became taut, as though in a clinch with Sully.

"Don't crush me, dear," she said— "heavens, what strength."

"I didn't mean to—I, I."

"I know," she brushed her hair back, "I was thinking of something just then, Shane—you're so nearly like Daddy—it's no wonder we both liked you right away." There was a pause during which her hands tried to encircle the muscle of his arm. "I believe," her words were vibrant, "that you can whip any man in the world." Her hands reached up to his immense jaws, the smooth fingers rubbing them, "And I want you to—remember, dear—Daddy didn't run when the locusts came."

She patted his cheek and was gone.

It was long before Shane, bewildered and confused, could say to himself, "Well I'll be damned."

XVIII

Late into the night the force of Shane's story still throbbed in her heart.

So many men had tried to caress her. And she had caressed him.

Before, she had been fond of him. Now—a great admiration came. He had carried everything within him. Events that would have marred others for life had made him strong.

He had not called his sister by name. She surged with feeling for the dead girl. Where had she read— the meaningless futility of human life?

What odds he had fought against! No wonder his jaws were set—his eyes so firm and old.

Her mother was astonished next morning as she entered the room, and walked toward Shane's picture.

"What will be next—is he *a prize-fighter now?*"

"And a good one," answered Lyndal. "I'm still very fond of him."

Her mother turned in alarm. "Tell me, Lyndal—you couldn't throw yourself away—oh, you couldn't, you couldn't—what do you know about him?"

"As much as you did of Father."

"But your father was not a—a—hobo."

"Neither is he—exactly—he has told me **everything** —I believe him."

"Have you told your father?"

"I don't have to tell him—he has known for a long time."

"But you are hardly out of college."

"You were only a year older when you married Father—besides—nothing has been said—he's very hurt —he needs someone with understanding—he's still quite a baby."

"I'd say a rather rough baby." Her mother looked grimly at the newspaper.

"You didn't find wings on Father."

Mrs. Lund looked admiringly at Lyndal. "What a lovely girl you are—what a prize for someone—but not for him."

"I'll be the judge of that."

"Why, Lyndal."

"Yes, Mother."

"You wouldn't do anything against my wishes."

"Don't be too certain."

"After all these years—a common hobo."

"I wouldn't say 'common,' Mother. He has a lot of character. He's never had a chance."

"He should make his chance."

"He's doing it."

Lyndal stood before her. "Mother—I've never done anything to hurt you—and I hope I never will. I've never been awfully fond of anyone before. I don't see much difference between him and my father— and I can't say more for him. He doesn't pretend— and he's sincere—that means a lot to me."

She looked in the mirror and began to brush her hair.

"Your lives have been so different," said her mother.

"That may be—but I'm never so happy as when I'm with him—and I remember Daddy Denmark saying long ago that it didn't make much difference where you were—it was according to who was with you."

"All right." Her mother left the room hastily.

"Something's happening to Lyndal," she said to her husband.

"What?" asked Peter Lund.

"She's still interested in young Rory."

"Why, that's all right—I've always liked him."

"But," pursued Mrs. Lund, "we know nothing about him."

"What do you want to know? He's a good worker —that's enough—I've been watchin' him. She might go further and do worse. He's a better man than that bug-catcher over'n Fargo you're so hot about."

"Why, Peter!"

"I believe in letting her alone. I have faith in her. You can't make beds for people if they don't want to sleep in 'em." He looked at his bewildered wife. "No one wanted you to marry me, did they—and I was fifteen years older'n you—cheer up, Mother—she's never caused us an hour's worry yet."

"I know," she said, "it would break my heart if she began now—besides—we knew each other—we were part of everything."

"They know each other." Old Peter glanced at the clock— "Let her live her own life—she's the best damn man around here."

"Don't be profane, Peter."

"Oh, hell!"

"Why, Peter!"

"Hell again!"

Mrs. Lund spoke quickly. "Suppose they married —and had a child—and he ran away."

"Who—him or the kid?" Peter Lund grinned.

"No good can come of it—no good—no good," she half sobbed.

"She's of age," reminded her husband— "She's got Grandmother's money. What can you do about it?"

A thought came to Mrs. Lund.

She sighed with relief.

There was to be a class reunion in Grand Forks. Lyndal would go.

Her mother was right.

Lyndal had another reason for going to Grand Forks.

A great decision had come to her. Professor Rogers would understand.

She had tried to love him. Once, when she had gone to her father, bewildered about him, he had said, "His head's full of echo wisdom." She had not forgotten.

"I'll be back Sunday," she said to Shane.

He watched her powerful roadster go down the road.

She had never been so happy.

Soon after she had gone, Mrs. Lund sent for Shane.

Quite casually she brought the conversation around to Lyndal.

"It seems like only yesterday she was a little girl,"

she said, "and now she is on her way to be married to a young man in Grand Forks."

No blow in the ring had been so hard.

"She's known Professor Rogers so long—he taught her in school. They have so much in common. I'm sure she would never be happy with anyone else—"

He turned away. There was no anger. It was not his world. He knew it years before.

What difference did it make—slug-nutty or not, he would return to Silent Tim Haney and the ring.

Alert with anticipation, Lyndal drove swiftly toward home.

The farm was never more serene when she arrived.

Norway and Sweden followed her to the head-quarters of the hired men.

"Is Shane there?" she asked.

"No, Miss Lund, he left yisterday."

She took a quick breath, and hurried to her mother. "What has happened?"

"I don't understand."

"He has gone—are you sure?"

She saw her daughter's expression. "He left sud-denly—that is all I know. One can never tell about such men—they come and go like the wind."

"Mother," her voice broke, "I'll never—" a look of desolation stopped the words. Her lips trembled. Her hands went to her eyes. The words ended in a sobbing torrent. "He was like Daddy—strong and simple and sweet."

The mother looked at her daughter.

"Did you see Professor Rogers?"

"Yes. I told him it was over—"

Before her mother could recover her surprise, she was gone.

A light gleamed from her father's room.

His arm went round her in that enormous sympathy born of understanding. "I don't know what to say. Nothing's worth your tears."

Heat lightning cut the sky. Under its slow flare the fields glistened a more vivid yellow. Thunder rolled with slight noise, like far-away empty wagons going down hill.

The harvest was soon over, and the harvesters gone their roving ways again.

XIX

Silent Tim Haney stared as Shane approached.

"Where've you been?" he asked.

"Never mind—I'm back."

"You see where you'd of been—where Sully is—champion of the world."

"It's not too late yet."

"Do you mean it?" asked Tim.

"Match me with anybody."

"We'll get you some clothes first." Tim eyed Shane, "then we'll start bombardin'—you can lick any man in the country—I'll give a story to the newspapers that you've been roughing it in the Oregon woods."

He took him to New York, and sent for Blinky Miller, who was now blind in one eye, oil of mustard having been rubbed into it from the glove of another fighter. "Keep him company, Blinky—and his mind busy," Silent Tim ordered. "I'll line up some warm-up fights for him."

Blinky nodded, as Tim added. "Say nothing to him —he might kick over the traces again."

"Okey."

Silent Tim went to a large suite of offices. There he talked to a man his own age, stern and hard as himself.

"Hello, Dan—"

"Why, hello Timothy—what brings you here so early in the morning?"

"Kindness, Dan—just kindness—I want to show you how to make a hundred thousand dollars."

"Is that all, Tim?"

"No less—and maybe more." Tim's eyes gleamed with a half smile. "You wouldn't be one to be refusin' money—would you, Dan?"

"Ah, Timothy, the man who'd refuse money you'd give would be a darin' man, indeed."

"How strange you talk—for a man whose walls I've papered with money—but we know each other too long to worry—I have a great boy, Dan, the greatest in the world—he's a million dollar fiddle with a ten cent string in him—you know all about him—Shane Rory."

"Yes," nodded Dan.

"As you know, Dan—some men are born like stallions in a parade—the harder you hold them the prouder they prance, their manes high and their nostrils wide and their iron shoes strikin' sparks from the pavement."

"Yes, yes, Timothy."

"Well, he's one of the stallions and I need your help."

"How?"

"I want to send him on a barnstormin' trip—six good men in Portland, Seattle, 'Frisco, Los Angeles, Chicago and Cleveland. It's a build-up for the championship—everyone of them has to dive—and Rory can't know it—he's one of those funny fellows—an honest Mick."

"Too bad," said Dan, "too very bad."

"It is that—he carries his own cross, Dan, and there's splinters in it bigger'n your arm."

"Well, Tim—"

"I know—ten percent of money up to ten thousand." Tim saw Dan frown. "Well, I'll raise it ten percent all the way."

Dan played with his watch chain.

"It's ten percent of a million or two, Danny."

"All right, Tim—let's see—we've got Leo Harvey in Portland—a win over him would make the headlines—Billy Randolph in Seattle, and Joe Mankerlitz has Barney McCoy in 'Frisco, and Billy Weil has Slugger Regan in Los Angeles. I'll make the schedule."

"That's fine, Dan—and by the time it's over we can move in against Bangor Lang and Torpedo Jones— enough wins will make him forget his cracked jaw and his loss to Sully."

"That's right. We'll not fail, Tim—we never have."

"And we won't now—just as sure as your name's Daniel Muldowney."

"We'll make it legal, Tim—ten percent straight through—if you have bad luck in any of them towns I'll deduct mine. It's not chicken feed I want."

"I know that, Dan."

Harvey and Randolph went down and out on schedule. People began to talk of Rory's comeback.

Instead of going down in six rounds, Barney McCoy fought viciously, and had Silent Tim worried. He glanced at Mankerlitz across the ring.

When Shane answered the gong for the seventh, Tim whispered to Blinky, "It's a cross."

McCoy slashed across the ring, the ancient grudge of Cheyenne in his eyes.

"He's settlin' down," sighed Tim, as Rory countered twice; "five rounds after this one."

Straining every nerve, Shane knocked McCoy out in the eleventh.

Late that night Silent Tim Haney telephoned Daniel Muldowney.

"Rory did not win until the eleventh, Dan. We thought he might win in the sixth."

"Thank you, Tim—we'll take McCoy off the circuit. Good night to you."

Blinky Miller entered. "I've just put him to bed. He was grittin' his teeth—he don't love McCoy—he told me how he double-crossed him in Omaha."

"In Omaha—what about tonight?" He sighed. "Ah, Blinky—it's gettin' so you can't trust your own mother in the fight game. It'll be hard pickin' for McCoy from now on—a man's word's his word—but we'll never peep—the papers might get it, and if we ever got a guy like Hot and Cold Daily sore he'd ride us forever."

The talk of the sporting world, Shane arrived in Los Angeles. Dilly Dally met him at the train. Pictures were taken of the meeting. An engagement was rumored in the newspapers.

"Gee, I just knew you were goin' places. That's why I gave you up," she explained. "What about that other girl?"

"What other girl?" asked Shane.

"You know—the one you told me about."

"Oh, her—I don't remember." Then, "How are things comin' with you?"

"Oh, good. I worked four days last week—a boy friend is lawyer for one of the studios—he gets me in."

"That's fine." The old lure for her was strong as ever. "What's his name?"

"Mr. Jonah Goldfinger," she replied. "I'll introduce you to him—he's not jealous."

"All right," said Shane. "A lawyer, huh?"

"Yes—a big firm—his father and his uncle and his brother and another man."

"Gosh," said Shane. "If they all got after a fellow."

Tim came upon them in the lobby of a Hollywood hotel.

"When did you meet her?"

"A couple of days ago."

"You're lyin' in your soul, Shane—and to them that have your good at heart. There's more floozies in this town than cattle in the stockyard. They graduate here —get their almer maters from small towns, as it were. But a bad girl's like a bad fighter, Shane—they always think they're winnin'."

"I know," said Shane.

"No, you don't, or you wouldn't be talkin' to them in hotels."

One of the largest crowds in the history of California pugilism saw his fight with Slugger Regan.

Amid thunderous applause Regan went to the canvas in three rounds.

Winning his next two fights on schedule, he reached

New York, where his six recent victories over outstanding men were used by Silent Tim to excellent advantage.

Daniel Muldowney, president of the Outdoor Association for the Advancement of Athletics, stated in an interview that Rory was the logical contender for the heavyweight crown.

Sully's manager pointed to Rory's two defeats by the champion, and insisted that he fight Bangor Lang. He disposed of him with, "He'll never get by Lang."

"If we do, do we get Sully?" asked Tim.

"After you fight Torpedo Jones."

"But Sully didn't beat him."

"He's champion—and our terms go."

"You're a nice fellow, Al—an honor to the game," Silent Tim sneered.

"I'm lookin' after my fighter."

"You'd better."

A match was made with Lang.

"A broken jaw's always stronger when it heals," Silent Tim assured Shane. "Besides, you'll draw a million dollar gate and Sully'll have to fight you if you win."

"Joe Slack'll be in his corner," informed Blinky Miller.

"That'll help none," said Tim, "Slack can't fight his fight—they think because he fought me four times he knows what I taught you—Joe could whip any man in the world but me—he was a great fighter."

"You were born too soon," Shane smiled.

"Or Joe Slack too late," returned Tim, "He was the best man I ever fought—but that won't help Lang now."

Nearly as tall as Shane, Lang had been champion five years.

"I'll be sorry to beat you, Shane," he said before the fight.

"Don't worry about me, Bangor," Shane smiled grimly, "or my jaw either."

"All right—" Too big for the rancours of the ring, Bangor held out his hand, "I can think of a million men I'd rather whip."

"So can I, Bangor." Shane shook his hand.

"I'd say 'good luck,' Shane, but you'd know I didn't mean it."

"So would I," laughed Shane.

Their manner changed in the ring.

During the first round, Shane's left shoulder was nearly paralyzed in blocking a wicked right counter. Shane remembered his broken jaw. In the last ten seconds he landed the hardest punch of the round, scoring a left under Lang's heart.

"That got him," exclaimed a ringsider.

Lang's knees buckled. The audience became tense. When the gong sounded, the ex-champion started for the wrong corner. Shane good-naturedly turned him around and patted his shoulder.

Lang was hardly off his chair in the second when he was aiming with deadly accuracy at Shane's once broken jaw. Three times his blows crashed. Shane smiled and danced away. They exchanged blows again. Lang landed a hard left to the jaw. Shane took it smiling.

Lang's surprise was not over before Shane was inside, slamming the great fighter's anatomy as if it were a drum. Lang went to his knee, and touched the floor with his glove. The referee began to count.

Lang shook his head.

The roar of the crowd made it hard for him to hear.

Sully sat at the ringside, an alert expression on his face.

Joe Slack "accidentally" hit the gong with a cane. A dispute arose.

Silent Tim glowered at his ancient enemy.

"G'wan—take care of your palooka—he needs it," Joe Slack sneered.

Silent Tim returned, "You callin' your betters a palooka when you never could fight a lick."

By the time it ended, Lang was himself again.

With ice applied to the back of his neck, and smelling salts to his nose for a minute, he whipped out of his corner as the bell rang and beat Shane to the punch with a right cross to the jaw.

"He'll break his jaw again," a voice thundered, as another right blazed through Shane's guard. He "rolled" with the punch. For an instant Lang was off-guard.

Shane crashed with a right, and Bangor's knees doubled in pain.

A left uppercut caught him. He thudded to the canvas, out for ten minutes.

Shane went to Lang's dressing-room. The once great champion lay on a cot, his face turned to the wall.

He sobbed several times. He had lost a chance to regain a world. It was all he had.

Hearing Shane's name, he stood up.

"We're even, Shane—here's my hand."

"Thanks, Bangor—take care of that eye."

"I will—I'll have a lot of time—I'm hanging up the gloves forever."

He rubbed the long muscle of his powerful right arm, and looked at his conqueror kindly.

"When you feel something leaving you, Shane, and you know it's the years takin' the dynamite from your hands till all that's left is a shell, it's time to say good-bye—"

"What do you mean—'the dynamite from your hands?'" Shane felt his jaw.

"Well I lacked something—you got me."

"You were mighty fast, Bangor."

"But you slowed me up by takin' all I had and givin' me more."

"It's been swell knowin' you, Bangor, and that's the truth—if you ever need anything—"

"Not me, Shane, thank God—I can eat dirt—I own land."

"I was a tramp kid when I first heard of you, Bangor."

The ex-champion laughed, "And if I hadn't saved my money you'd of made a tramp out of me—but watch yourself, Shane, against Sully—he's a great fighter—don't let 'em fool you."

"Thanks, Bangor. So long."

"One more hurdle," said Silent Tim, "and we filled the stadium." He sighed, "Thank God we're by Lang."

"You're right—he paralyzed me with that right to the jaw." Shane's hand went upward. "Trying to keep him from connecting I seemed to bump right into his glove."

"He'd be dangerous at eighty," mused Silent Tim. "He feinted for your heart and aimed at your jaw— a foxy fighter—"

"He's a nice fellow though," said Shane.

"Yes, Bangor's all right—fightin' was his business, and he fought like a man— 'Never get mad at a news- paperman,' he used to say. When Hot and Cold Daily was sore at him, he got drunk and called Bangor's suite from the lobby of the hotel. 'I'm coming up, Bangor, and take the championship away from you.'

" 'All right,' says Bangor, 'but bring it back in the morning. I'll need it when I fight Sully.'

" 'How are you goin' to hate a guy like that?' says Hot and Cold Daily."

XX

Shane was sent against Torpedo Jones—the winner to meet Sully.

When the match was made, Silent Tim, knowing he was on dangerous ground, said to Blinky Miller, "Torpedo's the only man ever to whip Sully—it's too bad—but if Shane can't beat the Nigger he'll never be champion—it's the game."

The words, "It's the game," covered for Silent Tim all the misfortunes of life. Did a man die when the heavens of happiness were opening, or a Jerry Wayne wabble out of a courtroom, demented, it was all "the game" to Silent Tim.

"Daily'll smoke us hard—in his heart he don't think we can get over Jones—and, after all—he's a newspaper-man—he's got to be as tough with words as Shane is with gloves—people have to get on—just why, God knows."

"That's right, Boss," agreed Blinky.

Under the heading,

RORY MATCHED WITH SULLY

and in smaller type . . .

If He Defeats Jones

Hot and Cold Daily wrote one of the columns that made him the most widely read writer on pugilism in the world. Combining the technique of the sideshow spieler with a flare for drama, he began:

"It's the battle of the ages, the black gorilla and the white chimpanzee, the winner to hurl his mighty mallets of pain against the champion of the world. Make no mistake about it, Shane Rory meets a great fighter in Torpedo Jones.

"There's different kinds of smartness in the world, and in that ring the black gorilla's as smart as Shakespeare.

"Torpedo Jones is a reincarnation of four wonderful colored men of other days—Joe Gans, Sam Langford, Jack Johnson, and Jack Blackburn.

"He's all of them rolled into a smirch of livid, illuminating, devastating power and skill. He has all of their good points and none of their defects. A powerful fistic machine, his coördination is perfect—a hair-trigger brain impulsing muscular action into flashing and deadly slaughter.

"Those old time Negro battlers developed a fighting system known as 'tailing.' It is now obsolete in sport vernacular because the bruisers of the old days are no more. Torpedo Jones is the first great 'tailing' fighter in twenty years.

"To 'tail' means to keep close to a foe and be a constant target until he is forced to slash away. The instant he makes a move to drive in with a blow, the tailer beats him to it with a punch that travels but a short distance. His blow is given added force because the foe is coming in fast toward it.

"Tailing is now called counter-punching. It is more

effective than that. The Black had it instinctively, and Torpedo Jones is the crux, the master, the quintessence of them all. Rory's manager, Silent Tim Haney, should know this. He fought Sam Langford a memorable draw when the black man was coming and he was going.

"Most boxers must pull back fist and arm to get a punch started. That's the exact instant Torpedo Jones starts a few of those twelve-inch laudanum-laden slashes of his.

"Stolid men of the Torpedo Jones type—stolid but not stupid—are of the deadly game order. If Torpedo Jones is knocked down, he will get up fighting, more dangerous than ever. If Rory knocks him down—then what?

"A battle with Torpedo Jones would test the courage and the strength of a gorilla.

"He is at his peak now. Great fighting men reach such a peak but once—and Shane Rory is meeting a great fighting man at that peak. If he has a lapse as he did with Sully, he's a gone goslin'.

"And more than that—Torpedo Jones is a savage on whom civilization rests no more securely than a shawl thrown over an old man's shoulders.

"He walks like an animal. He no more looks you in the eye than does a hyena. The expression on his face is sulky and sullen.

"He's as serious as a major operation—and far more deadly.

"His manner in the ring is that of a wounded wolf about to lose a bone.

"Even the lion can be trained to go to its stool when the act is over in the circus. The miracle is that Torpedo Jones can be sent to his corner when the bell rings.

"When an opening comes, he whips his blows so fast you can hear the crack of the punch before you know that one has been delivered.

"For the first time in twenty years, here is the perfect prize-fighter.

"He has everything—the cross-counter, the body pivot, the foot shift on the throwing of the right hand, the deadly jolting of a left jab, timed to the second, and every other trick that goes into the bag of a really great fighter.

"Are you sitting in a breeze, Mr. Rory? And is your heart not often as heavy as the world when you think of Torpedo Jones?

"It's the fight of the ages, Gentlemen, if Silent Tim Haney brings his machine gun."

Silent Tim folded the paper with the comment to Blinky, "Daily's buildin' us up by knockin' us down— a perfect newspaper guy. I'll show it to Shane—it'll burn him—and that'll help."

After Shane had glanced at the newspaper, Silent Tim said, "You're a smart fighter now—remember the night you fought Sully the first time. Go in that way. Never stop swingin'. Don't think about counter-punchin'. Punch so fast he can't counter. You'll never knock Torpedo out defendin' yourself. You're the greatest fighter in the world. You can't study a fight with Jones—you may as well try to dodge bullets from a gun. Go right out when the bell rings. The best man in this fight's the one that's up when the other's down."

"That's good advice, Champ," Blinky said. "Don't spar with a cannon. Just shoot harder'n swifter. You can take him." Blinky was confident.

Late that night, Daniel Muldowney and Silent Tim met.

"Daily sent the odds on Shane down to two to one. You'd better have him play up Rory—we can't hurt the gate."

"All right, Timothy— Will your boy win?"

"Ask me something easy, Dan—like which came first, the hen or the egg . . ."

XXI

Berniece leaned over Hot and Cold Daily. "I got your message, Big Boy—here I am."

"That's swell, Pal—better beat it back to your seat —he's got a lot on his mind right now."

"Will he win?" she asked anxiously.

"I don't know—it'll be a great brawl. He's fightin' the greatest man in the world—he's got to be right —beat it, Kid—they're coming."

Waves of cheering followed.

His face immobile as an ebony mask, the Negro was first to enter the ring. His green silk bathrobe removed, his powerful bronze muscles slid, smooth as quicksilver and ominous as doom.

He worked his tremendous shoulders before the robe was thrown across them.

Blinky Miller jumped into the ring and held the ropes apart. Shane followed.

His eyes rested on Torpedo Jones.

Silent Tim's hand was on his shoulder. Belying the turmoil in his heart, he smiled, "Just go in, boy. I'm in your corner." Though his words expressed invincible faith, he bit his lower lip to keep it from twitching.

Oblivious of all around her, Berniece watched Shane.

How different he was now. He looked downward

as the gloves were laced on his hands. From then on, he looked at nothing but his antagonist.

"Good luck, Shane," Hot and Cold Daily shouted. Shane's head went up and down. His eyes did not move. They were still set when the cameras clicked.

Blinky Miller, with Shane's name knitted in large yellow letters on the back of his red sweater, was busy in the ring. "I'm not goin' to let 'em think I'm with the other guy," was his explanation.

After instructions were given, a man yelled, "Where's your machine gun, Haney?" Hot and Cold Daily smiled.

Shane went to his corner.

"Go right-hand crazy like we told you," said Blinky Miller, "but only when the goin's so rough he'll think you're too tired to punch. Get all you got behind it."

Silent Tim nodded.

The gong rang. Bullet-swift, Rory turned, and faced his mighty chocolate-colored foe. The Negro's hands were hardly up before Rory's gloves struck with the hiss of angry snakes.

"He's got him! He's got him!" Mighty shouts went up. The great Negro danced from the avalanche of punches like a dummy on a string.

The thud of blows could be heard many rows from the ring.

In flashing seconds, the Negro was rubber-legged and bloody. He could not get set. It was the Rory of old before him. His gloves, the color of Torpedo's body, sank into it. The Negro's knees sagged from the fury of the punches. He circled around in the roaring clamor. The furious Rory was upon him. Hot and Cold Daily was oblivious of everything but the whirling brown and white bruisers. Rory's gloves were everywhere.

"He's down! He's down!" the audience screamed. Rory was in his corner before the echo of the gong died away.

"Good work, Champ—he can't take 'em and live." Blinky Miller held Shane's tights loose around his muscle lined body.

"Stand right up at the gong," commanded Tim, "Get set and wait—he'll come like a cyclone."

Torpedo dashed from his corner. Rory met him. For thirty seconds blows were traded even. Gloves missed each other and connected in a wild delirium.

Torpedo missed an uppercut. With tremendous effort he stopped the sizzling blow before it had traveled six inches upward. It was too late. For a half-second his guard was open. Swift as a maniac farmer swinging a scythe, Rory chopped a right. Cracking Torpedo in the solar plexus, it doubled his body to the shape of the letter U, and sat him on his haunches so hard he bounced.

"Oh, my God!" A reporter slapped Hot and Cold Daily on the back.

"Cut that stuff. We're not in the ring," snapped Daily.

Shane rushed to a neutral corner. Relentless as destiny and cruel as fire, the murderous Negro was upon him. His muscular brown back glistened with water. Frenzy rose in waves on the fury that followed.

Silent Tim's hands were tight shut. Hot and Cold Daily stared as though chaos had come. Was this the merciful Rory?

Berniece leaned forward, lovely as dawn, her eyes clear as early dew.

Neither man backed up. Eighteen inches apart, they volleyed and rolled with punches.

"Oh, oh." A man at the ring collapsed, clutching at his heart.

"A doctor here," yelled a reporter.

They carried the collapsed man away.

Suddenly Rory stopped and held both gloves to his chin. Torpedo lashed with a right and a left. Swishing around and downward went Rory's right again like a madman. Jones took the body-crushing blow, doubled up, and came back slashing.

"He didn't get him, he didn't get him! Lord, what now!" Hot and Cold Daily might have been yelling against the wind.

Now began that measured something that is beyond description, that made of the two magnificient bruisers the most perfect machines on earth. Blows went through openings narrow as cracks, swift as light. Each face was firm set, the eyes fixed. Masters of the art of destruction—one had to give way.

A left and a right caught Rory. Shaken as a lightning-shivered oak, he went back. Whirling blows, jabs and hooks followed. Rory was against the post of the ring.

With legs firm as rods, he slashed back at the terrible brown bruiser before him.

Blood-bespattered, he broke clear, danced to the right, skipped to the left, and was inside the Negro's guard. Torpedo retreated before the wild and terrible tornado. The audience was numbed into silence, as the furious givers and takers of pain, with lips tight shut, stood toe to toe, and battered each other with blows that shook the ring.

"It can't last—it can't last!" Hot and Cold Daily eased his heart with the words.

The gong rang fiercely. Neither man heard. The referee dodged low between and broke them. The fighters dashed to their corners.

They came out swiftly, chins low, mighty shoulders bowed, wet and blood-soaked, sledge-hammer fists ready to strike.

As though each were jerked by the same wire, they began at once to volley. Rory suddenly shifted, weaved in and out. When Torpedo made ready to counter, he was upon him again.

"Now watch Torpedo!" shouted Hot and Cold Daily.

They whirled madly into Rory's corner. "Break his heart—break his heart, Shaney." Tim's words went through the ropes— "The scythe, the scythe, the scythe—the scythe!"

Like tops spun madly, they whirled into the center of the ring. Both went to their knees, got up, volleyed, and went down again. They got up again, connected with blows and went down with trembling knees.

The referee began to count between them. At seven, Torpedo struggled and squirmed and got one knee off the floor—then sank again.

Tears came to the eyes of Silent Tim Haney.

"Ah, Mother of God, Mother of God—" he muttered.

"Take it easy, Tim, take it easy." Daniel Muldowney touched his arm.

Blinky Miller gripped the lower rope.

Rory was up at nine, staggering weakly. The indomitable soul of the great Negro struggled within him on the floor. His arms moved, his legs jerked spasmodically. His body was unequal to the call of his unconquerable spirit. Taking the full count, the mighty, proud, swaggering black man was carried to his corner still unconscious.

Blinky Miller hugged Shane. Silent Tim mumbled something to Daniel Muldowney.

"It's the greatest upset in years," said the radio announcer. "It was a spectacle for the gods."

"Well, a guy can't pick 'em all," Hot and Cold Daily smiled as he entered Shane's dressing-room with a group of other reporters.

"He didn't do bad for a two-to-one shot, did he, Daily?" Silent Tim Haney adjusted Shane's silk scarf.

"Not at all, Tim," replied Hot and Cold Daily.

"It was that right that circled around and down that got him," a reporter commented.

"We thought it would," smiled Shane, looking at Blinky Miller.

"What do you think of Torpedo?" asked Hot and Cold Daily.

"He's a fine fighter—the best yet," answered Shane.

"Better than Sully?" followed Daily.

"I don't know," returned Shane, "Sully's champ."

A white-bearded old man touched Shane's arm.

"You don't remember me, do you?" he asked.

"No, I don't," replied Shane.

"You came to my hotel after you fought Harry Sully. You were very ill—and I took care of you."

"Is that so?" Silent Tim Haney listened indifferently.

"Well, what can I do for you?"

"Oh, nothing," replied the old fellow—"You forgot to pay your bill and you had no baggage."

"What was the bill?" Silent Tim Haney asked.

"Four dollars."

"Well, here's ten." Tim handed him a bill.

"Thank you indeed. So honest a man's sure to have good luck." The old man walked away.

"Are you sure he runs a hotel?" Silent Tim's tone was sarcastic.

"What's the difference?" asked Shane. "He needed the dough bad enough to ask for it."

A half-dozen men emerged from the dressing-room of Torpedo Jones. Walking slowly, with heads down, the light slanting across them, they were weary and slow-moving. The last to pass Shane was Torpedo Jones. He looked at his conqueror.

"Ain't I seen you before?"

"Sure," replied Shane, touching his arm, "that rainy night in the railroad yards."

"Oh yeah, and you give me fifty cents—Lawdy, boy, you took it back tonight. So long."

He moved away with the sinister and powerful grace of the young victor in the battle royal.

It was his first defeat.

XXII

Blinky Miller was long silent. "I never saw nothin' like it, Boss," he said at last to Silent Tim, as though Shane were not present. "A guy thinks nobody kin beat a guy and along comes a better guy. I don't think no one ever lived could beat Torpedo but him. I couldn't believe it after he was out."

"Neither could I," smiled Shane. "Every time I started that right it seemed like it burned his eyes with matches."

"Well, if we ever fight him again they'll put a million on the line for a guarantee."

Shane put an arm about the frowning Tim.

"Sure—if *we* ever fight him again," he laughed.

"Well, his punches hurt me too—every time he landed I could feel the pain."

Daily and Berniece joined them.

Shane bowed bashfully and smiled. Blinky Miller did likewise.

"Your sweater fascinated me, Blinky," Berniece laughed. "How'd you ever come to pick yellow and red?"

"Tim done it—I wanted lavender, and he said I wouldn't look good in lavender."

"Let's all have a snack," suggested Hot and Cold Daily.

"Sure—I'll sing for you." Berniece took Silent Tim's arm. He drew back as though she were a hornet.

"No," he said, "We'd better turn in—the boy's had a hard day."

"But you can stay up a little later now," she looked toward Shane, "his hardest day's over."

"All but one," put in Hot and Cold Daily. "Come on, Tim, my story's in. I call you the greatest manager of all time—let's go." He motioned for a taxi.

"But you ribbed us hard before the fight—readin' you, a fellow'd of thought Torpedo threw mountains around like pebbles."

"It built the fight, didn't it—and it's all forgotten as yesterday's headline tomorrow—the only privilege a newspaperman has is to contradict himself— We've both got to get by, Tim. You wouldn't see Daily starve, would you?"

"Well not all at once," Silent Tim's lips curved.

Blinky, his mind still on the fight, looked at Silent Tim and said again as though Shane were not present, "Sully can't beat him the way he fought tonight, Boss."

Silent Tim took up the words, "Of course Sully can't beat him. The man to beat him isn't in the world right now—and it's a big doubt that he was here before us. They say too much of the old timers—it makes talk for schoolboys—Shane would of knocked John L. Sullivan's head over a cloud—and Bob Fitzsimmons —ho-ho—a man that a rassling mauler like Jeffries could whip would have no chance with Shane."

Silent Tim turned his eyes from Hot and Cold Daily to Shane. "There's never been but one man who could fight like Shane. They called him the Dublin Slasher. He was square all over like a man carved out of rock. He never stopped swingin', never backed up—and he had his own science in the ring. He knew every inch of rope, and every foot of canvas. He could tell within thirty seconds when the bell would end the round. And in them thirty seconds he could whip a bull.

"He was a graceful fighter, and his gloves were swords. In the ring there was nothin' like him—a kind of genius when the gong rang—always he came shufflin' to you, his right foot scrapin' the floor—he knew it was to brace himself. He could of found an opening in a crack for his fist to smash through. He was always on top of you like a shadow with gloves. I've seen him make great fighters cry. If you got an advantage for a minute, he'd top you in time to take the round. He was just a cyclone that moved like a slow wind—it's something you can't explain. You couldn't make a move but that he'd beat you to it. And he was never tired or flustered. I watched his hair when he fought. If the other fellow mussed it up he'd smooth it down with his glove when the gong rang.

"I brought him over here and the New York bunch tried to steal him. He was loyal, for an Irishman"—Hot and Cold Daily smiled—"and when he wouldn't break with me they began to frame him on a trumped-up charge that he wasn't no more guilty of than a baby. But one lawyer's enough to hang a saint—and they had five.

"If he wouldn't fight under their control, he

wouldn't fight at all. It was too bad—but it's the game they call the manly art.

"His mother was a very proud woman, God rest her soul. He didn't seem to care about himself—just her. She was pious and proud, a bad combination—she cracked and died—and something died in the Dublin Slasher too—but he was strong in his head like his body—and it came to life again—there's men that walk when they're dead, and the Dublin Slasher's one of them. And so—with many thousands of dollars —we beat the rap—and the Dublin Slasher went right on slashin'."

Hot and Cold Daily looked out of the taxi window. "It's a great story, Tim—I want to write it some day."

Silent Tim chuckled. "When your grandmother becomes a virgin again."

"Why Tim—you wouldn't imply that I wasn't honest?"

"No—not that—you just contradict yourself."

A faint smile touched Shane's eyes, as, with folded arms and tight lips, he gazed straight head.

Blinky Miller looked at Berniece.

"Ah yes," went on Tim in half reverie, "He was a broth of a boy—as weak as water and strong as a broken dam."

His eyes were softer as they strayed to the girl, "Always a ladies' man was the Slasher. He'd follow a skirt all day—and now, where he is, they're as useless as a pocket in a shroud." A slight twinkle came to his eyes, "But I wouldn't be sure. On a warm night, when the moon is soft and lingers with its shadow on the grave of a pretty maiden—well, the Dublin Slasher may find his way there—for he'll always be walkin' through the valleys at night with his boxin' gloves on his hands, lookin' for a rose about to bloom in the mornin'.

"When he was a lad in Enniskillen, he was loved by a lass—before he went on his thunderin' way—he didn't take her with him—bein' confident he could pick up another girl when he got there. She cried a little. The tears mended her heart so it could break again. Her name was Ruby.

"The Slasher wanted to go to a little place in the West where the mountains rolled away like ridges on a custard pie when it's old.

"The waters would help him, he said—it was like the lightnin' goin' to a garage for new batteries—but I said nothin'.

"Time hung heavy as a loaded glove in the place—for the peace was in the mountains and not in the poor Slasher's heart. And God help us till the day we die—there was a girl there—and that was enough for the Slasher. She was the sweetheart of some Eytalian warbler who played music in the dining-room so the guests couldn't eat too much—but the Slasher didn't believe that other men owned women. He just thought they were put around the world like roses—and the man up first got them before the dew fell off their petals. So he was cavortin' just like the big Saint Bernard puppy he was with the young maiden—when the Eytalian sees them—and may God never allow any more misery in the world if what I tell you is not true—that Eytalian shot the great Slasher with a little Flobert rifle. You wouldn't have thought it possible—such a tiny bullet endin' such a mighty man—like a rain-drop floodin' a mountain.

"I took him to New York, as lonesome a trip as a man ever had. At such times a man wonders what the meaning of it all is.

"When I got him to New York the very men who'd framed him were givin' him a send-off. I was wishin' that God would lift him out of the coffin to smack them over.

"The undertaker met us, and I'll never forget him. He was sympathetic as a second in the other corner. He was runnin' for some office in the gift of the people. Undertakin' wasn't his reg'lar business any more except when a big shot died and he'd get his name in the papers along with the dead. His face was like a lamp with no light and as empty of oil as a gourd. He had the mock reverence of a cat when it's killed the wrong mouse.

"We all sat around in the room with the undertaker sayin', 'Make yourselves comfortable, gentlemen,'— and all of us starin' at the box that was loaded with him that would niver get out—

"And Joe Slack says, 'He was a good fighter—almost as good as the men of the old days.'

" 'Ah nuts,' says I, 'Joe, you're always talkin' of the old days. Wasn't it you and me that fought four times long before this dead lad was on the way to his mother's womb— You know in your very soul that this boy would of fought us both in the same ring till our ears dropped off—don't let your mind get old by sayin' there's no good men walkin' the earth in these days.'

"And Joe said, 'Have your own way—I didn't agree with you in the old days, and I don't now.'

" 'It wasn't us that made the decisions—it was the referee'— But I said no more—after all, it's not fair to fight old battles over the great dead.

"Then a drunk reporter comes in, and 'God rest the soul of the immortal Slasher,' says he.

" 'God rest your own soul,' says I—'it was you that helped to break his heart.'

"The reporter starts to laughin'— 'Why, Tim,' says he, 'not even God can give rest to what a man ain't got' — He staggered towards the coffin— 'Suppose we see what the Dublin Slasher looks like—after all.'

"The undertaker has two young undertakers with wing collars and black ties open the box.

"While they were takin' the lid off, the reporter says to me, 'Tim, you better have someone warn Jack Dolan'—and everybody laughs.

"Jack Dolan was the good fighter the Dublin Slasher beat so bad—rockin' his ribs so loose he was never the same again—

"And when we were all quiet the reporter says, 'Don't let nobody ring a bell when the lid's off—he'll hop right outta that coffin and sprinkle us all with embalmin' fluid.'

"Well, when the lid's off, we all look down—I'd seen him so often when the blood was runnin' in his veins like fire—but I'd never seen him quite like this before—

"His fists were closed over his breast together like a

young priest prayin'. His head was square as a block and his jaws were so tight together you could see the muscles bulge. It was just like he was sayin': 'They'll never hold me here.'

"A crucifix and a rosary was wrapped around his hands like they was afraid he'd start hittin'—and his shoulders just fit into the coffin. And there he was so still a baby could slap him.

"The look of him sobered the reporter. He made the sign of the cross on himself and says something in Latin.

" 'Pray United States,' says Joe Slack—'to hell with all that Greek.'

"We'll let him lie in state here, as it were, for a while,' says the undertaker— 'He'll rest easier with all your kind thoughts flowin' over him.'

"Handsome Ed Barney'd been his trainer. He had a big nose—and he stood there wonderin' what it was all about, and the tears slid down his nose as he wondered—

"We started the Slasher to the boat at last—and there never was such a congregation of riffraff since the mad world began—men who'd of shot you for a quarter, wept like babies over a lost toy—and forget-me-nots who'd of been nice to a hangman were innocent little girls again. Someone played some music by a fellow called Chopang—and when we got in sight of the boat, Joe Slack said, 'I'm damn glad it's a big one—if the Dublin Slasher takes a notion to roll over it might list the ship.'

"The band was blarin' and rasslers and fighters and reporters and other thugs mixed their tears and their laughter with pimps and gamblers and lovers of the manly art—along with saloon keepers and priests and bums and other prominent people."

Berniece watched Shane.

"It was hot work followin' our fighter on his last journey to Ireland—and I couldn't help thinkin' that out of the roses on his grave, a big tree might grow—for there'd be no use bringin' a man to such perfiction and throwin' him away like a burned stick in the night.

"Well, that was the end of the Dublin Slasher—oh well, it's lovely weather outside—and a short night till morning—peace comes then with bullets in his guns."

The taxi stopped at a crossing.

"It's hell," said Hot and Cold Daily, after a long silence.

Berniece glanced sideways at Shane, whose hand went across his forehead.

"It is that," agreed Tim, "and may the sun never wither the weeds on his grave."

"Gee—a tough break," from Blinky Miller.

"He was a great fighter." Hot and Cold Daily looked at Berniece as if to have his words confirmed.

"He was that," agreed Silent Tim. "There was never none greater." His eyes met Hot and Cold Daily's. "But it's all in the game," he concluded. "The ring's too big for just one referee, else he'd never of counted the Dublin Slasher out so young."

Silent Tim put a hand on Shane's knee. "And I almost forgot," he said. "The other girl's name was Ruby."

Hot and Cold Daily sighed, "I'd say it was a case of too much Ruby—"

Silent Tim looked scornfully at him. "You'd joke in your grave," he said.

XXIII

When they were alone, Hot and Cold Daily said, "I've never pulled a fast one on you yet, have I, Tim?"

"Well, some that were not so slow."

"Then we're even—remember the one you pulled after the fight between Blinky Miller and Jerry Wayne?"

"I can't say as I do—mine is a busy life." Tim's head shook. "It must have been long ago—poor Jerry!"

"Well, you made a prime sucker out of me. I still remember it."

Silent Tim smiled.

As a young fellow, Daily reported the fight Jerry Wayne had with Blinky Miller.

No decision was given. Thousands of dollars were wagered on the result.

There was a hot dispute as to which had won.

Quietly, Silent Tim approached young Daily. "Who do you think won, me lad?"

"Why, Jerry Wayne by a mile, and I intend to say so out loud in *The Bulletin* tomorrow."

"You're a young man, but a shrewd judge of fighters," Tim said.

Pleased, the callow young reporter left.

Tim joined the vociferous gamblers.

"Well, of course," he drawled some time later, "I

have five thousand on my own man—and Jerry had that much on himself. I want to show my faith in the leading newspaper. I'll pay my money on *The Bulletin's* decision—and so will Jerry—"

"That's a go," responded several gamblers in unison.

Not till long afterward did Hot and Cold Daily learn how Silent Tim Haney had used him.

"You don't remember, huh?"

"No, indeed not—I made it an early rule at the beginning of a turbulent life never to remember an injury."

Hot and Cold Daily exploded, "Well, I'll be damned. Anyhow, we'll skip it, Tim. I just want to convince you I'm on the level."

"What'll it cost?" Tim asked.

"Not a red cent. I just want you to encourage your boy to see all he can of Berniece Burue. It'll do him good."

"And why, may I ask?"

"Well, you can't keep him caged up forever like a bomb on the way to explode—if you'd had her he wouldn't of run away the other time."

"He was in the Oregon woods."

"That's what you say, but I'll never double-cross you, Tim."

"I'll never believe it till you die without doin' it," Tim said with warmth.

"Why do you always think the worst of people?"

"I don't," answered Tim, "they're just what they are. But if you think the worst, you're generally right. I wouldn't be mad at Shane for havin' big muscles, or you a pug nose."

"We'll let my nose ride—I'm asking you to encourage Shane with this girl. He needs her."

"Do you remember Jerry Wayne?" came Tim's incisive question. "Well, he married a girl—and may I never rest easy in my grave if I ever forgive her—that awful little pimple on a great man's heart—she was born for the preliminary stumble-bum she finally married— but first she married Jerry, long enough to kill his soul and have a funeral for it every day—so she and her damned sparrow friends could sing like crows over it —I know I shouldn't blame her, but damn her, I do— and I will if I live to be a million—if I ever feel myself gettin' cool about her, I'll jump in the fire of the rotten memory of her and get hot all over again."

As a newspaperman, Hot and Cold Daily knew that the best stories were those he dared not write.

Silent Tim continued, "You forgive your enemy so he can sharpen his knife, and no quarrel is ever made up; so I'll have no more of her."

"But don't judge 'em all alike—this gal's different."

"A different dress, maybe, but still the same—and look what happened to the Dublin Slasher—a big tree cut down because he had a bird in his head—a fine growin' lad who'd of been heavyweight champion."

"Well, Tim, you won't trust me, eh? I could have crucified your fighter in the paper."

"I can say nothing to that. If it'll make you sleep well, you can go ahead and print whatever you like— but if you do—the arm of God will never be around you—either here or hereafter— He'd scorn you here, and it'd be too hot for Him there."

"It's a good story, Tim—and my job's to write."

"Yes, yes—somebody must clean the streets—and you may as well rake the gutter of your brain as the next man—you don't dare tell the story—your mother's ghost—if you weren't hatched out of a buzzard's egg—would haunt you."

"But, Tim—don't take it so seriously. It's like you say—all in the game."

"The heart of a great man like Shane should be in the game—a man who can crack a blow as quick as the flick of a tiger's paw—he should be above your little rapsacality—and you'd tie a skirt to him, like the tail of a kite in a still wind—an eagle with lead wings lookin' dreary at the sky. Shane wants no such woman—what could she bring him—the latest tune from a song-writer's vacant brain. He can make stronger music by the swish of his gloves. Why, you're not married your-self, and all you have to do is wring the diapers of your mind—and you get paid for it—and the boobs read your pother as though you knew what you were writin' about—why, you're nothin' but a lookin' glass—and all that's in you is the thoughts and doin's of bigger and braver men."

There was a smile in Hot and Cold Daily's eye. "But, Tim, why lambast me?—you'd think I was Joe Slack."

"My God, you braggart, of course you're not Joe Slack. Why you'd rattle in his skin. Jaysus Christ—if you say so—"

"But now listen, Tim, let the girl be close to him. The white velvet in the night—a rainbow in the morning—why you can't keep a girl like that away from him."

"Ho, ho—'white velvet in the night'—you talk like a poet with a floozy in your head. Men never win fights when there's too much white velvet in the night—let them have the dames who have nothin' to do—but a fighter who gallivants with gloves and who crashes a man like Bangor Lang to the floor—tell me, damn your Daily soul—what can he have to say to a butterfly with a skirt?"

"Well, many a good man falls for them—look at Napoleon—" Hot and Cold Daily's eyes were lit with humor.

"You look at him—the puny little runt! Shane Rory could of spanked him before every battle—huh—you think of the half-men—"

"Jim Corbett liked women."

"A dancer with gloves—jabbin' and runnin' backwards—what could he do with men like Rory and Jones, who punch and go in till they either knock a building down or know what's holdin' it up." He grunted with disgust— "That ham, Corbett, with his ring-around-the-rosy in the ring—a nance weighin' two hundred."

"But Corbett always spoke well of you."

Silent Tim jerked his head in surprise. "Why the hell shouldn't he? I never did a Romeo in the ring—and 'twas not from my example a lot of sunken-chested fairies begun to flit about with gloves."

"But Jim was a decent fellow, Tim."

"I'm not sayin' a word about him as a man—except

that he wasn't much good as a fighter—why his seconds had to carry a big lookin' glass in the ring—he even complained that Kid McCoy hit him too hard."

"There was a good man—McCoy."

"Yes—he was the livin' argument against women," Silent Tim frowned. "And it's my job under Heaven to protect Shane Rory."

"For fifty percent," put in Hot and Cold Daily.

"You're lyin' as you sit, Hoten Cold. Sure, I must live, the same as you, unfortunately—but if you can tell me that according to my own lights I ever pointed a finger or deserted a friend, I'll buy the candles for your funeral—gladly."

"All right—never pointed a finger, huh? How about Barney McCoy?"

"That's different—he did a Benedict Arnold. I'd rather point a gun at him than a finger."

"I don't suppose you ever crossed anybody up." Daily's eyes had a touch of mirth.

"Never—when I give my word."

"The hell of it is, you never give your word, Tim."

"You're right, a man's word's his lantern in the dark —it should not be lightly given."

He glanced out of the window.

"Will you let me out at the Royal, I have a late talk on with Daniel Muldowney."

"Sure thing, give the old rascal my love," responded Daily.

"And what would he be doin' with your love?" asked Tim.

"You can't tell," laughed Daily.

"Good night, you scalawag, you woman lover," Tim said testily.

With slow step and solemn expression, he went into the building.

"Good evening, Daniel."

"Good evening to you, Tim. What's on your heavy mind this night?"

"The weight of the world, Daniel—I've been carryin' it since mornin'."

"Put down the load in your old friend's hands, Timothy. It's no time to weight yourself down when you're so near the home stretch—with the greatest man in the world."

"And the wildest," cut in Tim.

"Never mind that—if he wasn't that he'd be something else. Gawd, I'd give me soul in hell to punch like him."

"But I got a sad letter this mornin'," said Tim.

"Oh we're all gettin' sad letters—they make the mail slow."

"But mine was from some lawyers."

For a fleeting second a glint of steel came into Daniel Muldowney's eyes.

"Lawyers—trouble?"

"Yes, Dan, four lawyers."

"And what's it about?"

"The boy."

"You mean our Shaney?"

"Yes, Daniel."

"Four lawyers," Muldowney snapped the words, "Who are they?"

"Goldfinger, Goldfinger, Goldfinger and Riley."

Muldowney smiled. "That last fellow must be a Jew."

"You may be right, Daniel—but there's one Irishman there, I know—there's trouble. I know them all—I mean these lawyers."

"Where are they located?"

"Los Angeles."

"And what's the trouble?"

"It seems that Shaney deported or imported, or some damn thing, a girl from Cheyenne to Frisco and stayed there with her for no moral purpose—her name is Dilly Dally."

Again Daniel Muldowney smiled.

"Can you import a gal with a name like that?"

"Yes, I saw the little bitch with him in Hollywood."

"And was she purty?"

"Yes, damn her soul," replied Tim. "And what can we do, Daniel?" His eyes narrowed, his jaws clicked, "Nothin' will stop me now."

As if to soothe a terrible tension, he lapsed into the ancient Irish habit of smoothing it with velvet. Softly he said, "I know this Mr. Riley— Ah, Daniel, he's a snake on a rock and the warm sun shinin', he's quiet as down and glib as a sparrow losin' a worm. There's an eternal justice, Daniel—it's higher than the mountains and lower than the sea—if you do evil, it floats on the wind and strangles you for breath."

Daniel Muldowney's words broke in with a dolorous croon, "Take it easy, Tim, take it easy—they may stretch the rope but they'll never hang the boy."

Daniel Muldowney rose, and cracked the next words like a whip, "remember that!"

"I will, Daniel, I will. You see, I've learned to like the boy—I don't want to see him suffer." His voice rose, "They can put him in the penitentiary for that."

"He's not there yet, Tim."

Daniel Muldowney fell into a large leather chair and stared at the millions of lights below. Himself an Australian jailbird at twenty-three, wrestler, bruiser, politician—the ruler of his world—ruthless, relentless and dew-soft, according to the mood or the occasion, he had from his fortieth year not seen the day he could not comand ten million dollars.

When breaking in as a promoter, a rival said, "This'll cost you a million a year."

"I'll last ten years," he said.

Tim did not disturb the silence, but gazed over Muldowney's shoulder.

"I was just thinkin', Tim, how long we've known each other."

"Yes, Dan—nearly thirty-seven years."

"We've had nothin' and everything, Tim, but the most we've had is we understand each other so's we can talk with our eyes and they don't know what we're sayin'. I remember the first time we met—I didn't have enough money in the house to pay the other fighter—you took one look at me and said, 'I'll put in the rest of the purse and fight him for you. I like the cut of your jib'—I'll never forget that, Timothy."

"And neither will I, Daniel—the fellow nearly knocked me down with a sucker punch—and then we all got pinched."

The two wealthy hoodlums chuckled.

"But those lawyers, Timothy—what did they say?"

"They'd give Mr. Rory four weeks to answer—they wanted no unpleasantness—the girl had suffered greatly as a result of this journey—but they did not wish to worry Mr. Rory at this critical stage of his career. And then a gentleman called today and said that perhaps the whole matter could be settled for a few hundred thousand dollars."

"Ho, ho," chuckled Muldowney. "You can build a pyramid for that."

"Of course, Daniel—I'd rather pay you than lawyers."

"I know you would, Tim—it's not money now, it's justice—the boy's done no wrong. A floozy over a State line—and to pay such money or go to jail for that. Why I'd sneak one into heaven—but why did he take her?"

"God knows," replied Tim. "You can get a club woman for nothin' in most towns."

"Well, do nothin' Tim—let Blinky watch the boy— if it goes to trial, it'll cost a fortune—and some simple thing like that'll crack the boy's career—we can't have it, Tim."

"I know, Daniel, if they crack a suit, he'll lose to

Sully—he's that high geared. I saw the Dublin Slasher break."

"What a boy! what a boy!" crooned Daniel Muldowney. "It's our duty, Tim, to save such lads—the world needs its fighters."

"It does that," returned Tim.

"Can I have the letter, Timothy?"

"Yes, Dan."

He put it in his pocket, saying, "Goldfinger, Goldfinger, Goldfinger and Riley," and then, "let's have some coffee, Tim. It's not two o'clock, and I'm afraid I'll get sleepy."

XXIV

Daily and Berniece met at the Royal Hotel.

"Does he still think I'll vamp his fighter?" asked Berniece.

"Oh, yes—everything's one color to Tim."

He led her to a table, "But he'll get over it."

He watched her eyes. "Cheer up, Kid, everybody gets hit once. You'll get over it by the time it touches your heart."

"Why do you say that—do you think I'm that cold?" she asked.

"Not exactly." Hot and Cold Daily was silent a moment before he asked, "Why do certain types of women go for fighters?"

"What do you mean—*certain types*—I've known a dozen fighters and you've never seen me excited."

"That's right—stopped again. I will say he's different." He took his elbows from the table. "And, my God, how he can fight—I didn't think a panther could lick Jones as quick as he did."

"And yet he's like a child—maybe that's the combination women like."

"They like every combination they can't work." He leaned back.

Berniece smiled whimsically. "For a fellow who knows so much, you know so little," she said. "I knew if I ever met him I'd go for him—my dad used to talk so much about him, I guess. I'd do more for him than his manager—if he'd only understand."

"Well, you'd never make Tim understand. He's of the old school—women are poison to fighters and that's that—but I'll help you meet Rory now and then."

His belligerent chin dropped. With an effort, it was firm again. He looked straight at her.

"Do you know much about men?"

"I think I do."

"Well, you don't—no woman does; all the little surface tricks, maybe."

She frowned prettily, pondering the words. "Maybe you're right."

"Now let me tell you something, kid—get this first—memorize it—there's nobody smarter than Mrs. Daily's pug-nosed son."

Berniece smiled. "It's marvelous the way you hate yourself."

"You mean the way I know myself. But anyhow, get this—I got a tip from the coast—a little girl out there was all set to take Rory for a ride—Old Tim doesn't know I know it. Well, she went off a cliff in an automobile. You see, kid, if Tim's not dumb, neither's Rory. Blinky Miller trusts me—it's funny, some people do—I know a newspaperman's a louse and a what have you, but he's human, and if one of them's your friend —well anyhow, Blinky told me that after Rory sent the money to bury the little punk, he said to him, 'that little devil would of framed me some day—I've been expectin' it ever since I got in the money'—so you see, he's not so dumb. He met this gal in a restaurant, took her to Frisco from Cheyenne before he joined Haney. You see, baby, newspapermen and God are the only people who know everything. You can't get your head up as high as Rory's without guys like us peggin' you —that's our business."

"Well, well, I suppose you also know who the other girl is—the one with a name like a Pullman car, Mr. Solomon?"

"Yes, Berniece—but that's a private affair. When a man cracks up, it's not a matter of record in our books. But we know it—we'd be suckers if we didn't. Old Tim pullin' that Oregon woods stuff! Everybody in this world's got to talk to somebody. Rory's committed no crime, and if his heart's heavy and Old Tim freezes him up, what's more natural than talkin' to Blinky Miller, and Blinky half the time is as unconscious as a city editor—so one night he told me where Rory'd been. I got on the 'phone and sent a Minneapolis man out to peg the story—and boy, it would make your heart ache —and the girl—with the name like the Pullman car— she has to talk to someone also—and of all the people in the world, to an old Danish washer-woman with para- lyzed ankles. Our man can't move in on her, so we send a young Dane cub to work the old racket—peddlin' chromos. He shuffles a few pictures of people in the neighborhood till he comes to this girl's; he goes back and forth—and we get the story—all in Danish. He brings a picture of Rory in fightin' togs—she knew him, you know, and the young Dane says, 'you know he's part Dane.' I think that's a lie—he's part Norwegian, I think—but no matter, she told the story—and I think it's the damnedest thing I ever heard.

"The old lady lives in a three-room shack near the Grainsville stockyards. Everything's supplied her by the girl's people—and she's closer to the girl than anybody, except her father—and it's another Tim Haney and Rory affair—the fighter spills his heart to Blinky and the girl does to the old lady. I didn't know there was a love story left in the world, but, by God, there's one. The old lady saw her come roarin' down the road in a big yellow roadster and stop, then come hurrying in sobbing, 'Oh, Granny, Granny, hold me, Granny.' The old lady kept cold towels on her forehead, and the girl kept mumblin' all the time, 'My baby—my baby.' I suppose meanin' the guy who paralyzed Torpedo Jones—if you figure women out you can pass on into heaven—you're too bright for this world. The kid met her, sellin' chromos. He says she's beautiful as hell."

Berniece shuddered; Daily resumed, "He'd been there four or five years before—he was a husky, good-lookin' kid, and he reminded her of her dad, and she got stuck on him. He got to be kind of like a body servant. She went to college and he breezed away without sayin' a word. Then he floats back after he blew the fight to Sully. It started all over again. Then she goes out of town to tell some high-powered gink it was all off—that she was coming back to Rory, a wheat-tosser on the farm, hidin' out, and when she got there he was gone. Anyhow, old lady Jorgensen kept the girl with her a day and a night before she'd go home—and then Mrs. Jorgensen had to go with her. It's a little jumbled the way I tell it—but you get the drift of the thing.

"The picture of that old Danish washer-woman, big around as a barrel, and hobblin' on paralyzed ankles, lettin' that girl sob herself to sleep in her arms has got anything licked I ever heard of. I remember lookin' at him, and me drunk as an owl on sacred wine—and thinkin' 'what a handsome, big bruiser you are' and me lecturin' him like he was a kid because he blew to Sully —you know, I write doggerel for pastime—it keeps me from writin' poetry. I wrote about the Dublin Slasher:

> It's all a riddle we cannot guess,
> No more than they of Ancient Greece—
> But a sculptor modeled you nevertheless,
> And wrecked his greatest masterpiece."

Berniece looked up, "That's nice."

"I'll say."

He motioned for a waiter.

"When I think of those two punks whipped around like a couple of doves in a gale, it makes my heart ache. I often wonder who started the whole business any-how. It might have been Tim Haney—but the boys out Minneapolis way tell me this gal's a lolapalooza. She's made Rory suffer. He don't know it, for that's all he knows—what a hell of a miracle he is—Jack Gill told me about him out in Kansas when he was just a tramp fighter. Everybody in the camp liked him the first day. He was Gill's sparring partner—in the first clinch he said in Gill's ear, 'Can I throw 'em?' Can you imagine that—and Gill, a champion? Gill said 'yes' quick and stepped back, and he told me he was damned lucky he did—the kid went to work. Gill liked him so much he moved him in on Buck Logan over in Omaha—well there's not enough snow in the mountains to make a whiter man than Buck was—and Rory was like his son. You know, I meet all the boys—and most of the girls—I guess it's because I'm a sympathetic cuss. I just look at every man and say to myself, 'Gee, he's got to die,' and right away I'm sorry.

"When Bangor Lang fought him the second time, he tells me Rory said to him, 'Bangor, if I lose to you, I won't be too sorry—you were swell to me after you cracked my jaw'—you see, Rory's got a left jab that's strong as a pile driver. I'm telling you it *would* knock an ox down—he hunches over and moves it up and down and pushes it out. If it lands solid, you go down —well, he got Bangor. When Bangor got up, Rory moved in for the kill. 'I was never hit so hard and often in my life,' said Bangor. 'It was like razors cutting through my brain.' And when it was over Rory said, 'I thought it was the decent thing to do, Bangor; Hot and Cold Daily told me I had too much mercy with Sully.' "

Daily's mind was crossed with a fleeting wonder at life.

"How long have I known you, Berniece?"

"Too long—five years—I was nearly eighteen when I had the misfortune to meet you."

He laughed, "Come to think of it, I've never seen you dissipate."

"And you never will either—women can't drink—it's like pouring nitro-glycerine in a cream puff, and then lighting it."

With a sudden shift, "So your dad used to know Rory's, huh—did he ever tell you what he was like?"

"Yes—he liked him—a big, good-looking man, a stone-mason. Shane couldn't have been fourteen when he ran away West; no one ever heard of him till his name got in the papers—naturally when he got to be a good fighter, other neighbors remembered how bright he was—and all about his sister—people are like that—but my dad talked about him long before he was known."

"That's a great story. I'd like to write it—but it belongs in a novel—and I'm all in when I write a column."

"So am I when I read it."

Hot and Cold Daily chuckled. "How'd you happen to get in this racket?"

"Texas Guinan knew my mother and daddy. She's been like a mother to me. She took charge of everything when dad died—and all the bills. I paid her back, thank God."

"Tex, eh? White people!" Daily held his glass.

"I'll say so! What a world if everyone was like her," Berniece mused.

"You wouldn't want 'em all like her," Hot and Cold Daily put in; "it's just right as it is—with most of the world suckers. What the devil would a woman like Texas do if everybody was as smart as she was?"

"I hadn't thought of that," laughed Berniece. "They might smarten her up even more."

"She was a fine woman. She never let anybody down," said Hot and Cold Daily.

"And strict as a convent," returned her protégé. "But nobody knew it—she kept her soul in a private room—and she never let the suckers in."

Hot and Cold Daily half smiled, "What'll you do if you crack up from lovin' this guy?"

"No danger—the other girl met him first. Besides," with slight weariness, "my mother always said I'd never get any place till I found someone I couldn't have."

XXV

After a week's clamor in the newspapers, Shane was matched with Sully for the Heavyweight Championship of the World.

Silent Tim selected a training camp near a small lake in New Jersey, forty miles from New York.

The same cook had been at the camp for twenty years. In that time she had prepared meals for many famous pugilists. She called them "my boys."

Shane, with Blinky Miller, and two sparring partners, was introduced to her by Silent Tim Haney.

"You'll feed him well, now, Mother."

"Indeed I will—no man ever lost through my meals."

"They win in spite of 'em."

She laughed with Silent Tim.

The camp consisted of many buildings. At one end was an outdoor ring, surrounded by many tiers of wooden seats.

A small ticket window was nearby. Fifty cents was charged those who desired to watch the challenger train. A room containing typewriters and telegraph instruments for the use of newspapermen, overlooked the lake. A saloon and dance-hall was at the entrance.

Silent Tim had chosen Random Lake for several reasons, the principal one being it was free of expense. A celebrated fighter drew large crowds who spent money freely. All money taken at the ticket window went toward salaries for the sparring partners and other incidentals.

Satisfied with all, Silent Tim left Shane in Blinky's care. Before leaving for New York, he said,

"Make your mind up hard, Shane—and remember Sully has his own mind made up too—that's what makes a great fight. And remember again that Sully has the edge on the psychic stuff—there's a man in the world to get all our goats—and Sully's had yours twice—it's not how *you* figure—it's how *he* figures. It was me that sat an hour on the Dublin Slasher's bed before he fought Jack Dolan. It's the nerve strain you must watch. I saw the great Stanley Ketchell weep before his fight with Jack Johnson. He was a better man, but lighter. You and Sully are about the same weight. It'll be the last wild drive in you that'll win—and it's as much your heart as your mind—for you both can't cross on the same track—one of you's got to get off— and don't mind what the papers say about what Sully'll do to your jaw. Torpedo Jones didn't do it—lightning never strikes twice in the same place—I remember before the Slasher went in with Dolan—young Dolan had never been knocked out but once—a solar plexus—I had Wild Joe Ryan go to him and say, 'I'm givin' you a tip, Jack—watch your solar plexus—he'll play for you there.' It's all bunk, pay no attention to any of it— you've got to whip Sully—you've got to whip him if you're dead when you do it. He knows what you did to Jones—and Torpedo might of beat him—but Sully's still a harder nut for you to crack—it's the game—that's the way it goes, and no one's got the time to figure it all out. Sully may not be a better man than the Nigger, *but he is for you*, and you're the one that's fightin' him, and that makes all the difference. I can't watch your mind, but I can your body—and you'll be in the best shape of your life when you get inside the ropes with Sully."

Shane's heavy arm pulled Silent Tim to him, "All right, Grandma—now don't worry."

"My God," snapped Tim, "it's time to worry with a coupla million in your lap."

Tim had chosen wisely in Blinky.

No mother watched a sleeping child with more care than he did Shane. If the covers slipped from his shoulders, Blinky adjusted them.

He had the ego of a child and magnanimity not found in many greater men.

Why he was alive, or the forces that controlled his existence, were mysteries he did not consider. His life was made up of people and events connected with the ring.

He held no animosity toward Shane for the knockout long ago in Council Bluffs. He seemed to consider it an honor to have been beaten by so great a man. Though he fought Shane as a ringer, he had the knockout by him placed in his record. Other fights had followed. The record ended with "k.o. by Shane Rory."

Blinky's ears were shapeless. The muscles of his face were broken from the pounding of many gloves. Slightly punch-drunk, with a rasping voice, he was balmy as spring and gentle as a dying wind. Without the bitterness of defeat, like all those close to Rory, he became deeply attached to him.

Though Silent Tim Haney was often doleful as doom, Blinky was silent as sunlight when need be, and as cheerful.

He often mentioned the hundred dollars given him by Shane.

"Forget it, Blinky—it's the best investment I ever made."

"I'm glad you feel that way, Champ—there ain't no more like you. They've forgot how to make 'em."

In a few days he would again mention the money.

When Silent Tim Haney said to him jokingly, "You mighta licked Shane in your day,"—"Not the best two days I ever lived," returned Blinky.

Shane gave Blinky ten thousand dollars after the fight with Torpedo Jones.

Silent Tim groaned at the news. "You'll spend it in a week. Let me take care of it for you," he suggested.

"All right."

"You'll never see it again," Tim smiled.

"That's okeh—I've lost more in my time."

The words touched Tim, and he said, "It's yours though—here's my receipt."

"You keep that too—your word's all I want."

"Suppose I die?"

"Shane'll still be alive."

Each morning after his road work, Shane would have his "rub down" and breakfast.

He enjoyed the pounding and rubbing of his body,

and the odor of the soothing witch hazel that Blinky used. The one-eyed fighter's fingers had magic in them. While rubbing Shane's muscles, he would talk of different pugilists' weaknesses in disclosing an attack. "Jerry Wayne'd make his legs rigid, and then begin to dance . . . and always watch Torpedo Jones' left eye —Bangor Lang shifted before starting an uppercut—I don't know why. No matter how fast a guy is, his brain's got to be faster."

Sully was the master, the combination fighter and boxer, in Blinky's opinion. No one knew how or when he started a blow. Even in the heat of battle he left less to chance than any other fighter. Shane agreed with him. Yet Sully lost a close verdict to Torpedo Jones.

Shane would sit nude in the sun for twenty minutes. Blinky would then rub him with vinegar and oil and five minutes later soak his body in beef brine.

This gave him a tan that verged on black, and made his flesh tough as leather.

The newspapers contained many items concerning his deadly left hook. It was training camp strategy. His right was just as powerful.

He had learned one trick that few pugilists knew. It had won many victories for Silent Tim Haney.

If two men aimed with their right, both would land. It was even possible for them to knock each other out.

Shane had been taught to move his left foot four or five inches to the left as he threw his right. The blow meant for Shane's jaw would go over his shoulder, while Shane's would land with brain-jarring force.

"A smart fighter often falls for an old trick if he

thinks you're too smart to use it—maybe you can get
Sully to throwin' right hands—like you threw them
against Torpedo Jones," said Silent Tim.

"That's right," agreed Blinky Miller, "but don't try
it too early in the fight—his brain'll be too clear then."

XXVI

Sully's manager, Al Wilson, sat with the chief second in a cafe. A one-time acrobat with a circus, he became a spieler for a side-show. He found young Sully, a stake-driver, and developed him as a fighter.

Once muscular, Wilson had grown heavy. He had two chins, and pouches under his eyes. His jovial nature concealed a hard heart. He had but one idea. Money could do anything. He was only surprised at honesty.

"Well, how does it look, Al?" the chief second and trainer asked.

"Oh, so-so. If Sully gets over Rory, we've got easy sailin' for at least four years. There's no man around but Torpedo Jones, and we've drawn the color line," replied the manager. Then more deliberately, "But Rory's mighty tough."

"You mean,"—the chief second said no more.

"You get me—if Rory goes in there like he did against Torpedo Jones there's no two men on earth kin lick him."

"So what?" asked the chief second.

"Nothin'," returned the manager. "We need help—a bolt of lightnin' or somethin'."

"Well, Sully's a great man," said the chief second, "a damn great man."

199

Al Wilson paused. "The devil of it is, he may be meetin' a greater one." He lit a match with his thumbnail and puffed a cigarette before he continued. "You can prove anything in the fight game, and if I was on the other side I could come mighty near provin' that Shane Rory could lick any man that ever lived. He cracked Sully with a six-inch left on the windpipe the last round he fought him, and Sully nearly choked to death for an hour after the fight."

"I know," said the chief second, "wasn't I there?"

Wilson put the half burned cigarette on the ash tray. "And if we hadn't done business with the referee, he mighta give him the decision."

"I know," again said the chief second, "I'm shakin' yet."

Wilson took another cigarette.

"I've done a lot of thinkin' about fighters in my time—Rory's got everything—perfect synchronization. That's a million dollar word," he smiled. "His eyes and his feet, his hands, everything moves at once. He's better than Bangor Lang used to be at feintin' with his eyes—he's got that much contol."

The chief second broke in, "There's only one way to lick him."

"How?" asked the manager.

The chief second looked around, then answered, "Iron."

"You mean—"

"You know what I mean."

"How could you get away with it in a championship fight?"

"Nerve, and maybe a few grand to Blinky Miller," answered the chief second.

"They'd lynch you if they caught you."

"I know, but leave that to me." He raised his eyes. "Is it worth twenty-five grand to you?"

"Sure," replied the manager, "*if we win.*"

"You're funny," the chief second grinned. "The danger's in the loadin' whether we win or not," he said. "You can't take a chance on havin' Rory slaughter Sully—besides, I'll have to oil Blinky Miller's palm. Blinky and me are old pals, you know—he's crooked as a corkscrew."

"But we got the same referee we had in the other fight—Munger's okeh."

The chief second followed with, "He may be okeh, but he can't fight Sully's fight for him—if he goes down he's got to count ten sometime. And if Rory starts to puttin' him down, he'll stay there."

"That's right," said Al Wilson. "But he'll take a lot of chances on a long count for a hundred grand. He'll have to."

"It'll have to be a hell of a long count—and Rory'll murder the referee if he catches him."

The chief second took a kerchief from his pocket. Inside of it was a round piece of steel, about an inch in diameter and nearly three inches long.

The manager looked at the steel and asked, "Is it heavy enough?"

The chief second sneered, "Even if *you* had that in a glove you could kill a Percheron stallion—and just think what Sully'd do with it."

He wrapped the steel quickly in his kerchief. "They're all new gloves thrown in that ring, ain't they —well, you leave the rest to me." He paused—"*after you gimme the twenty-five grand.*"

"That's a lotta dough," Wilson said crisply.

"Sully's end'll be over a million," as crisply returned the chief second, "besides I'll have to pay Blinky."

"Suppose you get it in the wrong glove."

The chief second laughed, "Don't worry."

"All right," agreed the manager, "I'll come across."

"When?"

"Why after the fight—when we collect."

"No, no, now—I may not live till after the fight—if I get caught—Blinky'll want his in advance too. He's that smart."

"Well, what do you want me to do?" The manager was impatient.

The answer came quickly. "Go over to the bank with me and transfer twenty-five Gs to my account."

"Suppose it leaks out?"

"It'll be good publicity—you're givin' me that much to train your fighter."

The manager smiled, then wiped the perspiration from his forehead.

"You're fast, Billy," he said.

"I gotta be to get this over." His wrinkled face became set.

The chief second had been a featherweight fighter, but gave it up when the going got rough. His audacity earned him a national reputation as trainer and second.

The money turned over to him at the bank, he said

quickly, "Now, I want five Gs in the referee's pool."

Taken by surprise, the manager said, "All right."

A noted gambler on horses, the referee, Al Wilson, and several others had for years operated a gigantic betting scheme. "A guy's got half the breaks with the referee in his corner," Wilson always said.

When he found a referee who could not be "reached," Wilson was always fearful that the other side had got to him first.

Everything arranged, they returned to their apartment hotel. A bell-boy handed Wilson a package. It was for Sully.

"Open it," Wilson ordered the boy. The manager watched everything. A bomb might be sent to his fighter.

It was a new pair of green tights from Sully's sister. A skeleton head was woven on each leg.

"I've been thinkin', Billy," he threw the tights on a chair, "you've got to be prepared if you can't use the iron."

"Sure—that's all okeh—I got the plaster of Paris last week in Buffalo."

"Well, I got some too," put in the manager.

"Better hide yours," suggested the chief second.

Wilson went to a drawer and took out a small can. "You take care of it." He handed it to the chief second.

"I'll peek in on Sully," said Wilson.

"All right then—I'll look up Blinky Miller."

"Hello, Champ—how's tricks?" asked his manager.

"Oh, so-so."

Nude to the waist, his enormous muscles bulging, Sully was playing solitaire. "I nearly beat it the last time." He laid more cards on the table.

"How's the bettin'?" Sully asked.

"Ten to eight on you."

The champion chuckled. "There's still saps in the world who believe in that guy."

"Don't take him too easy," advised Wilson. "You gotta remember Torpedo Jones."

"Huh."

"And Bangor Lang," Wilson added.

"I softened Lang up for him."

"But who softened Jones up?"

"That's one of them things," answered Sully. "Rory's his jinx—and I'm Rory's— I'll bounce so many gloves off his chin he'll think it's hailin' rocks."

"That's the spirit." Wilson patted Sully's bare shoulders. "Better throw something over you."

XXVII

Shane's mind was in a whirl.

He would soon enter the ring for the heavyweight championship of the world. Silent Tim's words came to him, "And the world's damned big—there's a lot of good men in it." His hands went up and down the heavy ridges of muscles at his sides. His feeling of physical power was immense. He rose and stood before a long mirror. "I'll win, by God—" he said to himself, "all Hell can't stop me this time."

Sully had beaten him twice. It would never happen again. He threw his arms above his head. His muscles writhed.

"The first time was a fluke—the second was another —this is the rub-off." The words went through his mind.

"We're on our way, Champ," Blinky told him. "We can't lose now—remember how we took the powder out of Torpedo's keg—I just knew we'd take him."

All was plural with Blinky in connection with Shane.

Shane crossed to a divan; stretched motionless and stared at the ceiling.

Blinky sat in a huge chair, his hands gripping the side, his one good eye in Shane's direction.

"It's our big day, Blinky."

"That's right, Champ—I've got everything fixed.

The boss'll be here soon—you don't care if I take a little cat snooze—I gotta be in shape this afternoon."

"Go ahead, Blink."

Shane stood up, his wide shoulders towering above his trainer. "It's been a long road, eh Blink—but here we are." Their eyes roved around the elegant suite.

"All we need's ribbons, Champ," Blinky smiled, "and we'll get them after the fight—then the old gang can come here an' kiss us."

Blinky went to the room adjoining, "Now call me any time."

"Okeh, Blink."

The door closed.

He could hear the slight rumble of the city far below. Closing his right fist and hitting the palm of his left hand, then alternating, he walked about the room.

His greatest quality had always been the coördination of overwhelming courage with a will that could not accept defeat. He remembered as a road-kid watching a fox listen to the call of quails in a nearby meadow. It cocked its ears, and remained motionless as long as the quails called.

"A fox doesn't do that," an old Idaho trapper told him.

"But this one did."

Amazed at the boy's certainty, the trapper commented, laughing, "Well—it thought them quails was hoboes."

Shane applied the same quality to the ring. He knew by experience that under certain circumstances Sully was "a sucker for a right." He knew that Sully knew that he knew it. That Sully would train for weeks to overcome the weakness that no one was aware of but his greatest antagonist—Shane also knew. The plans of battle revolved in his mind. They would change under stress. "But I'll land that right." He practiced delivering the blow before a mirror.

One—two—one—two—one—two—swift and straight as bullets the blows swished through the air. But how to fool Sully. His brain was swifter than his muscles. So were Sully's. He knew.

Man to man, he could beat Sully. He felt it. But he had felt it twice before and lost. "To hell with those fights!"

Shane smiled grimly, remembering what Silent Tim had said to Hot and Cold Daily, "It's the last step that counts when you're climbin' a mountain—and Shane has the last step."

"If he don't stumble," bantered Hot and Cold Daily.

"He won't stumble—there's men who kin go so far —and there's them that can go the one step more—and that's Shane."

It would take the last step to beat Sully. He walked about the room.

Tim Haney knocked at the door.

"Are you hungry?" he asked.

Shane, hardly looking at him, said, "Yes."

Tim turned to the man with him. "Order breakfast from your room—they don't know you're with us— we'll take no chances on anyone slippin' dope in the food. Then bring it in here."

A glass of wine had brought Shane restful sleep

through the night. He knew instinctively that he was "on edge," but not overtrained.

"Well, how do you feel?" asked Silent Tim as the third man left.

"Never better," was the answer, slowly drawing a deep breath.

He threw a silk robe over Shane's muscular body.

Shane ate in silence, while Silent Tim glanced through the morning newspapers he had brought.

"The odds are even," he said, "It's a fool who wouldn't make you the favorite."

"I don't care who's favorite," Shane snapped. "No guy ever lived can lick me three times."

"But he didn't lick you the other times," Silent Tim cajoled.

"Well, they've got it that way in the record books— that's what counts." Shane's eyes roved over the city below.

"Where's Blinky?" his manager asked.

"He's getting a little sleep. He'll be here soon," Shane answered gruffly.

Silent Tim was pleased at Shane's mood.

"You can't lose, Shane." Old Tim was silent for a moment. "There's no man on earth can beat you this day."

As usual he hummed the same words:

> "On the road to Mandalay,
> Where the flyin' fishes play;
> And the dawn comes up like thunder
> Out of China 'cross the bay."

He turned to Shane, the wraith of a smile around his battered and hard old mouth, "Funny—I can niver git that line outta my head—'the dawn comin' up like thunder'—the very idea—how can it?"

"It'll thunder today." Shane moved his shoulders.

Silent Tim glanced at the newspaper nearest him. "Here's your measurements," he said. "You weigh 202 and Sully 204—his reach is 77, yours 78—"

"Huh," Shane grunted, "I've got it on him there."

Silent Tim read on. "His chest normal is 42—and yours 43½—more room for your lungs, me boy—and listen to this from Hot and Cold Daily's column.

" 'After watching the two fighters in training and considering those things that indicate one of the greatest contests of all recorded time, it is the opinion of this writer that it's either man up, and take your pick in the heavyweight championship of the world brawl this afternoon. No matter how terrible the pace set by either mighty antagonist, the other man will meet it. The writer concedes that Rory has lost twice to the champion in earlier days. He was then carefree, willynilly. There is now something else in his eyes. And who can ever forget his slashing and terrific defeat of Torpedo Jones?

" 'It is true that Sully has never been a flashy gymnasium fighter. He lacks the suppleness, the writer might even say the beauty, the grace and the glaring daring of the great and dauntless Rory—but it must be conceded that his training before the fight with Bangor Lang did not impress the onlookers. Yet he won the heavyweight championship of the world.

" 'A five mile run completed Rory's training yesterday, after punching the bag and shadow-boxing for twenty minutes.

" 'Both men are on edge. Both dislike and respect the other. Both are savage, gruelling, ruthless, relentless, brutal and terrible men. Both have brains as quick as a pickpocket's fingers. Both are primal and bitter. It is not likely that two such men will ever again meet at their peak. When I consider all the factors—I call it even-Steven—they are as evenly matched as two bullets in the same revolver.' "

Silent Tim shook his head in admiration. "Two bullets in the same revolver. He's not agin us, anyhow. If he could think like he writes he'd be a Harold Bell Wright—he can sling the words, indeed he can. But he'd steal your left eye and sell it for a marble."

He read another opinion.

" 'Great as the Rory attack will be—Sully's will be greater. If Rory could not whip the champion when they were both younger, how can he expect to do it now with the confidence and prestige of a championship behind Sully?' "

Silent Tim crumpled the paper. "What a fool he is to write that way."

"Who wrote it?" asked Shane.

"Joe Slack's name's signed to it, but never mind—he's a fool—now Hot and Cold Daily's a smart man—he thinks before he writes."

Shane picked up the paper.

" 'The vaunted Rory attack—with its wild flurry of

leather will not withstand the terrific assaults of the champion. Rory is a great heavyweight—ranking in the very first flight. But Harry Sully is greater. No man in the world can rate an even break with Sully fighting as he will fight today.' "

"We'll see," said Shane.

"The devil with that—what does a high school boy know about fights—even under Joe Slack's name?" Tim was indignant. "But this is better." He read aloud,

" 'Heavy demand for tickets to title bout— Gate expected to go beyond two million dollars.' " He put the paper down, saying, "I'll be leavin' you on a sweet note—you can rest a while before you weigh in—here's Blinky."

"Gosh, Champ—I couldn't sleep, so I went down in the lobby. I just heard Hoten Cold Daily bet ten dollars over in Jack's ticket office there wouldn't be a knockout inside of ten rounds."

"It was someone else's money," snapped Tim.

He looked at his watch, as Blinky went on, "It ain't eleven yet, and they're beginnin' to crowd out at the stadium already thicker'n thieves at a lawyer's funeral." He glanced at Shane's shoulders. "The sun's blazin' but that old beef brine in your hide'll turn it away." His voice rose as though he had just seen Shane, "How do you feel, Champ?"

"Never better."

"That's the stuff—take it easy—" Blinky's hand went over Shane's three days growth of beard. "Thataboy—they'll turn bullets."

"They'll have to," Silent Tim commented dryly.

"Gosh—you'd think the boss was in the other corner."

"I am—with a knife."

XXVIII

A pounding came to Shane's door.

Blinky listened. "It's some lost newspaper guys. There's a thousand in town from all over the world."

The voices soon subsided in the press headquarters. Smoking, eating, talking, drinking, a score of reporters lounged about in a large four-room suite.

A long table, loaded with food and liquor was in the middle of one room. Several waiters stood about ready to serve. Red and white banners with pictures of Sully and Shane were on the walls. In large black letters were the words,

"WORLD'S HEAVYWEIGHT CONTEST
15 ROUNDS"

Reporters came and went constantly. Between introductions and greetings, there was a continual hubbub.

"It'll be a dazzler today all right—hotter'n your ma's cook stove with biscuits in the oven," a weazened little reporter with faded blue eyes volunteered.

"Yeap," drawled another, "twilight in purgatory— and we poor devils working—oh well, the riddles of life and the ring are many."

"How'd you like to fight under this sun?" the first reporter asked.

"Okeh by me if I got a million bucks."

"But I'm telling you," a third reporter was over-heard, "Rory won't take all that Sully gives—he'll bring the saffron outta that guy just as sure's fog's in London."

"What do you mean—the saffron out of Rory?" asked the reporter with the faded blue eyes.

"Just what I said— I saw his second fight with Sully, and he wilted."

"Well, I saw him against Torpedo Jones. He'd carry all my dough if I had ten million." The reporter had not spoken before. "If he's yellow, then I'm color blind—"

"But Sully ain't Jones."

"I'll say he ain't—he don't belong in the same ring with Jones."

"That's what you think—I saw him go against Jones —the Nigger got the duke but I'd of called it even," again drawled the reporter who had talked about it being twilight in purgatory.

"Ho ho—Sully'll run him outta the ring." A new arrival reached for a drink.

"Well," snapped a blond reporter, with heavy jowls and defiant eyes,—"you're not asking me—but I'm telling you something—there's no guy on earth can make the Roaring Rory run—I know him longer'n he thinks I do—I worked on a little dinky paper in Wyoming when he fought there—they come in his dressing room—two of them—tall as pines and blue revolvers longer'n your arms— 'Sonny,' one of them says, 'you're a nice lookin' boy, and you got a lot of

years ahead of you—and we don't even know where
your folks are.'

" 'Well,' Rory says.

"And they says—'Oh nothing—a lot of the boys
have money on the McCoy and they'd be disappointed
if he lost.'

" 'What about the boys who bet on me?' asks Rory.

" 'Oh well—that's just too bad.'

" 'All right,' says Rory, 'have it your own way'—"
The reporter stopped talking.

"I told you he was yellow," a scribbler cut in.

"Well, what the hell happened?" two reporters
asked at once.

"Rory knocked McCoy out presto—he never once
looked at the guys with the guns—no siree,—I saw that
with my own two eyes—so nobody can tell me about
any yellow in that battlin' hombre. He may have too
much brains to want 'em scrambled—but he's not
yellow."

"Well,—there's another name for it," said the reporter who brought the charge. "There's something
wrong with him."

"Maybe he's got a streak of sensibility in him," said
the reporter with the faded blue eyes.

"Call it whatever you want, but he's got no business
in there with Sully with any kind of a streak."

"That's right," someone said.

The blond reporter sneered,—"You're all nuts—if
talk was money you'd be rich as Hearst—a fellow'd
think Rory was a palooka to hear you saps talk. What
do you think, Joe?" The reporter turned to a bat-

tered hulk of a man who poured whisky in black coffee.

"It's all Sully," came quickly from him.

"Let's feel your head," the blond reporter laughed. He was joined by the others. "The great Joe Slack picks another loser—why the devil can't an old time fighter pick a winner?" The blond reporter looked at Joe Slack, "Can you tell me?"

"I'm pickin' one," was the answer. "Sully'll hit Rory so hard you'll think he's shot from an airplane."

Laughter followed. Pleased with himself, the old fighter poured more whisky into his cup.

"Are you going to the fight, Joe?" a reporter asked.

"Sure—I got two ringside seats."

"Are you going twice?"

"Nope— I sold one ticket."

"How much?"

"Eighty bucks."

"How'd you get two tickets?"

"I'm reportin' the fight, ain't I? Don't I have a secretary?"

"That's right," returned the questioner, amid laughter.

"How'd you happen to get so much?"

"Eighty dollars for a fifty buck seat ain't so much when there ain't no more." The old fighter smiled crookedly at his questioner and said, "I wouldn't give eight bucks to see all the champeens that ever lived in a battle royal—no sir—not in a thousand years."

"It'll be a thousand years before you ever get eighty bucks again."

Joe Slack's cup shook as he chuckled. "Well, that may be—but I'm worth it—that's more'n I can say for a lot of word-slingers."

"That's right, Wood-Yard Kipling," spoke up a reporter, "when a guy gets too old to fight he always thinks he can write—you oughta be an editor."

"Oh I don't know," responded Joe Slack, "I get by all right— I can sleep nights."

All turned from Slack when a young reporter asked, "How heavy's the gloves?"

"Is it possible?" asked the blond reporter, "Your name just can't be Hot and Cold Daily—can it? You know just too much about the fight racket—the gloves weigh two pounds each."

"Don't let him kid you," another reporter said more kindly, "they're five ounces."

"Who're you coverin' this fight for, the *Sunday School Herald?*"

"Naw—*The Christian Science Monitor.*"

The laughter died away as Hot and Cold Daily and several other New York writers entered. With them was Jack Gill.

The other reporters were deferential.

"Make way for the big shots," the blond reporter said— "Hey, Mr. Daily—" he brought the young reporter before him, "Here's Damon Runyon, Junior, doing the big brawl for the *Youth's Companion.*"

Daily and his group greeted the youngster.

"Ever covered a fight like this before?" asked Daily.

"I never have."

"Well, you oughta do a good job—I'd like to see your story."

"Thanks, Mr. Daily."

"Don't mention it—if you get stuck in describin' the rounds—just say any old thing—nobody has 'em right anyhow—and the rest don't care." Hot and Cold Daily motioned to the waiter, "Give us some beer."

"I've got something stronger."

"Not in this heat—we've got to see the fight— Anybody goin' over to see 'em weigh in?" he asked.

"I guess not," replied the blond reporter, "Some of the fellows just left—the wires'll get it."

Daily turned to Gill. "Have a little beer, Jack."

"Nope—a small soda—some lemon in it."

"Who'll win, Jack?" the blond reporter asked.

"If it goes the limit—a draw—a knockout—God knows."

"Think Rory has a chance?"

The fighter turned.

"A chance—for cripes sake—he'd have a chance with a cyclone."

"You've known him a long time, ain't you, Jack?"

"Yep—he was my sparrin' partner—did a semi to me in Wichita—a dead right guy."

"Are you goin' to be in his corner?"

"If Tim wants me."

XXIX

Silent Tim entered Shane's suite.

"Get him ready, Blinky—it's time to weigh in—he's got to pass a physical examination." He looked at the rugged Shane. "You can't tell—he might be sick." Addressing him direct, "You're even money now, Shane—everything points to the biggest crowd in the history of the game."

"We can draw 'em." Blinky flustered about Shane, who glanced in the mirror. "All ready."

Silent Tim telephoned the clerk. "Tim Haney—car at the side door— Let's go."

"Now there'll be a crowd there, Shaney, what with the doctor and the commissioners and the politicians all wantin' their mugs in the paper—if Sully speaks, you speak—if he don't, you don't—any man knows what you say'll be said in the ring—with punches hard enough to make it rain."

Surrounded by photographers and reporters, the scales were at one end of the huge room. Shane followed Sully on the scales. "Two hundred and one— three pounds less—" reporters wrote hurriedly.

Sully glanced at the beam and started away.

"Pose for a picture." Wilson stopped him.

Shane stood near him as the cameras worked.

Neither man spoke.

Sully's chief second smiled at Blinky.

"Any statement, gentlemen?"

"We'll win," said Wilson.

"So'll we," from Silent Tim.

The champion and his manager were the first to leave for the arena. The fight was an hour away. On arriving, they went to the dressing-room assigned. Sully looked across the hallway. His adversary was just entering the building. Lithe, his jaws set, and walking swiftly, Shane raised his hand casually in token of greeting. Wilson glanced with narrow eyes.

As Shane stripped, the perspiration rolled from him. Blinky Miller looked and said, "That's swell."

The door of Sully's room closed, the chief second spread out all first aid medicine for cuts and wounds. Bandages were put on the table.

Wilson surveyed the chief second's work and said, "I'll mope on over to Rory's to see them bandage his hands."

"Okeh," returned the chief second; Then to Sully, "Sit down, Champ—take a load off your feet."

"I'm just lookin' in," said Wilson to Blinky Miller. He glanced casually at the soon-to-be bandages. "That's all right," he said, "I'll trust you fellows—walk over'n look at ours," he suggested to Blinky.

"All right." Blinky went to Sully's dressing-room and glanced at the roll of gauze and then across the table, saying,

"Okeh—go ahead." He left with unconcern.

The chief second worked hurriedly. Seizing a small pail of water, opening the plaster of Paris can, he put two tablespoonfuls in water and stirred with a small brush, while Sully wrapped the gauze bandages around his hands.

Soon the chief second painted the gauze. It began to absorb the solution. He applied another coat, saying, "It'll soon be like iron, Sully, old boy."

The fighter grunted.

The chief second took a roll of two-inch gauze and wrapped it over the hardening plaster of Paris. He then admired his work with a smile, while the plaster of Paris hardened.

They sat for some minutes. Wilson returned and surveyed Sully's bandaged hands and nodded approval.

"The first prelim's on," he said.

"It'll soon be over now," said the chief second, looking at the scowling Sully. "You'll knock that gazabo outta the stadium." He felt Sully's hands. "They're like cement."

A knock came to the door.

The chief second opened it. A uniformed usher handed him an envelope, and hurried across to Shane's dressing-room.

The paper read:

"Bandages to be applied in the ring—
The Boxing Commission."

The three exchanged glances, and Wilson said quickly— "What luck—"

The chief second cut the bandages. "I wonder if that one-eyed Miller crossed us."

Another knock came to the door.

Wilson opened it carefully. The roar of the audience could be heard.

"The second preliminary's on," an usher said.

"All right," snapped Wilson, slamming the door and turning to the chief second, "Miller's your pal, eh?"

Sully's hands bare, the bandages hidden, another knock came. Wilson opened it. Two newspaper writers entered.

"Well, how's your fighter?" asked a reporter.

"Never better, Edson," answered Wilson. "Get ready for a battle."

"What round'll the finish be in?"

"We're not saying—before eight though." Wilson looked at Sully.

"She's a fifteen rounder, and hot as a furnace."

"We know all about that," said Wilson.

"But you're goin' to know a lot more before you get through with Rory—all I'm tellin' you is to be ready for anything." Hot and Cold Daily was emphatic. "You'd better send Sully in there ready to fight'll his heart cracks—I wouldn't steer you wrong, Wilson."

"Thanks, old pal," said Wilson, adding, "We did it twice before."

The chief second threw a robe over Sully, who glanced at the woven image of the skull on his trunks.

Hot and Cold Daily sneered, "You mean you think you did it—ever hear of the imponderables?"

"What they got to do with fights?" asked Wilson.

"A damn sight more'n you think," returned Hot and Cold Daily.

A buzzer sounded.

"All right, we're ready," snapped Wilson.

Two men, wearing caps and sweaters, stood at the door.

"Bring everything, boys," commanded Wilson.

A voice droned, "Ready for the main event."

Sully, his three seconds, and Wilson filed past Shane's dressing room.

The newspapermen stopped at Shane's door.

The challenger was ready for the ring.

His trunks were tight-fitting. Long, snake-like muscles crawled around his body as he moved. His eyes had the hard glitter of murder.

The newspaper writers glanced with admiration at his nut-colored, powerful body.

"How's it going, Shane?" asked Hot and Cold Daily.

"You know," answered Shane.

An executioner was never more grim. From old custom he went first toward the ring.

"Good luck, Shane," said Hot and Cold Daily.

"Thanks, Buddy." Shane looked ahead.

"Is he goin' to win?" a bystander asked.

Blinky Miller rewarded him with a look of disdain. Then hurrying to follow the quick and powerful moving fighter, he threw back, "He'll die in there if he don't."

The reporters went to the press row.

"We're going to see a fight, eh," said Hot and Cold Daily to Jimmy Foster of the *World-Wide News Service.*

"It's in the air," Foster returned.

"It's in the bag," Daily chuckled, "There's no fake about this fight."

XXX

A wave of shadow passed over the crowd. A cloud slipped in front of the sun. It slanted downward with heat-shriveling force.

Airplanes, carrying trailers of advertising, droned overhead.

A subdued silence went over the mighty throng. A prolonged rumbling followed, like breakers on the sea.

"Here they are," a perspiring man shouted.

Neither fighter looked at the other, as he crossed to scrape his shoes in the resin.

The ring was crowded. The radio announcer talked hurriedly in the microphone. Every now and then his words were interspersed with the name of the firm that had given a fortune for the privilege of announcing the fight. Scores of newspaper writers greeted each other.

Over the audience, at fifty dollars a seat in the first hundred rows, were scattered the leaders in their different worlds.

Eight priests sat in a row, their benign faces in startling contrast to the turbulent, sun-scorched scene about them.

A battalion of huge, black and white clouds moved slowly up from the west and completely obscured the blazing sun for a moment. It burned through them, more appallingly hot than ever. A sprinkle of rain, not dried by the blazing sun, fell over the audience of a hundred and fifty thousand.

A box containing the new gloves was brought into the ring. The bandages were adjusted.

Managers and chief seconds handed them from one to the other. Sully's second took a pair and twisted them about, then stopped to wipe his face with a handkerchief. He quickly put the piece of linen in the neck of his collarless jersey shirt, and jammed his right hand into the glove. Taking his hand out and twisting the glove again, he fitted it on Sully's outstretched paw.

"Now's your chance," said Blinky Miller.

Tim Haney crossed the ring.

"Take the iron out quick—there'll be no fight till you do."

The chief second's eyes darted murder at Miller, who grinned.

Sully slumped on his chair, while manager and seconds crowded around him.

"Not getting away with the iron'll confuse 'em," Blinky whispered to Silent Tim.

The fighters posed for pictures. A dozen cameras clicked.

Shane looked defiantly in the champion's eyes. Sully met his gaze.

On the toss for corners, Shane got the one with the sun in his eyes.

Introductions over, the ring was quickly cleared.

Shane looked without seeing at the white mass of human faces.

"Ladies and gentlemen," the announcer's words thundered through immense trumpets in the wide roofless enclosure, "in this corner Dapper Dan Sully—heavyweight champeen of the world." He pointed dramatically. The roar of applause died away. "In this corner, Roaring Shane Rory—undisputed challenger—Marquis of Queensbury rules—fifteen rounds to a decision and the title."

Men and women stood on seats, yelling and clapping their hands.

"Down in front," came from many throats.

"Watch that Rory," a two hundred and fifty pound man confided to the stranger seated next to him. "When he begins to zoom them—boy—they zoom—Sully'll find it's just like slappin' a wolf in the face when he cracks him."

"Sully can zoom some too," the stranger cut in.

The fat man looked at him with polite scorn. He wiped his forehead with a large blue handkerchief, and did not talk for a moment. Instead, he began to drum wide knees with pudgy fingers.

The tension carried him away again. "Eventually Rory'll make Sully bring his guard down—and then his punches'll go zoomin' in like cannon balls shot by lightnin'." He looked sideways at the stranger, anticipating a dispute— "He's got fists that go so fast no one can see 'em— Did you see him drop Jones?" The stranger did not answer. "Well, I did—right then I said to myself, I said, 'Me for this fighter—he can knock a lion out with a pillow on his hands.'"

"You mean on the lion's hands?"

"No—I don't mean on the lion's hands—you know who I mean."

A band blared a fast tune.

"Good Lord, what a time for music—there's people who'd laugh at a weddin'." The fat man gazed scornfully in the direction of the noise.

"What's your name?" the stranger asked the fat man.

"Me—I'm Jeremiah Dodge—Chairman of the Maas Brewing Company. Here's my card."

"Thanks—I'm Joe Slack—one time middleweight champeen." The speaker grinned proudly.

The fat man looked in alarm. "Is that so—I remember—you were *some man.*"

"Yeap—we never got the millions in my day these fellows'll get—and we had to fight too—they were men in them days."

The fat man was now less certain of himself— "Now, of course, a man like you knows fights and fighters—and I wouldn't presume to talk to you like I would a stranger—why my father always said,— 'There'll never be another Joe Slack'— Now what do you think, Mr. Slack?"

"Well, I'll tell you—it'll be a dinger for a while—but Sully'll git him—Rory's fightin' things in there he can't hit—"

"He's mighty fast when he begins to zoom, though." The fat man was again reassuring.

"But you can't hit ghosts—I know—I've tried— Your fists go right through them."

The fat man looked surprised.

Joe Slack said no more. Putty ears, a flat nose, squirrel eyes, and a twisted mouth, he was known in the vernacular of the ring as "a good man in his day."

He stared at the ring.

Uneasy laughter, mingled with incessant low murmuring, could be heard.

"Just think," said a heavily dressed fellow, in spite of the weather, "this vast assemblage will all have passed from the earth in a hundred years."

"If this heat keeps up it'll be less'n that," was Jeremiah Dodge's rejoinder.

A silence of breathless expectancy followed. The stillness of dawn, a momentary hush, it lasted but a minute.

As if jerked in unison by a wire, three hundred thousand eyes turned toward the ring.

Hot and Cold Daily waved at Berniece, seated across from him.

XXXI

All became tense. The click of typewriters stopped at the ringside. Hands still ready to form words, the reporters looked upward at the fighters.

The referee called them to the center of the ring. They were formidable men. Sully was taller than Shane. As they now stood, with feet close together, they widened toward the shoulders in the shape of the letter V. Sully's hair was clipped close. Shane's was cut shorter than usual to keep it from his eyes. Each had several days' growth of beard.

Instructions given, their gloves touched. Standing, with muscles taut, they waited the gong in their corners.

Each fighter went forward when it rang.

Sully crouched and charged into Shane with lightning fury. He landed a right above Shane's eyes. It opened to the bone. He went down as though dropped from the sky. He got up at eight, still dazed, his body red with dripping blood.

The audience became tense. The referee's count could not be heard.

"Did you watch that glove?" Tim asked Blinky.

"It's okeh," answered Blinky, his eyes on Shane.

As Shane wobbled, another terrible right caught him high on the cheek. He went down again. His strong brain drove his body. With jaws firm set, he was up at seven.

Sully charged again.

Then came the mightiest transformation of all time in all rings. Like a master fencer, firm on his feet, his eye streaming blood, the left side of his face purple where Sully's blows had struck, the majestic bruiser sizzled rights and lefts with the deadly precision of machine-gun fire.

"My God—what a man!" A sports writer put his hands to his eyes.

"Cover, cover," shouted Wilson. Sully bounded from the ropes.

The huge audience roared.

Berniece clenched her hands.

Sully's brain raced.

Shane went down again from a short right to the wounded eye. The referee counted.

Shane did not move.

Sully rushed with swinging fists to answer the gong for the next round.

Wilson looked at Shane, then anxiously squinted at the slanting sun.

A powerful astringent congealed the blood above Shane's eye.

"Don't let 'em stop it," groaned Shane.

"Keep to his left," Silent Tim said, "Bury your jaw."

Blood-covered, lips puffed, eye half closed from Sully's terrific bombardment, Shane again pleaded with Silent Tim, "Don't let 'em stop it."

"I'll kill 'em if they do," snapped Silent Tim.

The gong rang. The champion rattled Shane's jaws with one-twos. He then worked downward to the stomach.

Shane doubled under the tornado of pain. The champion's jaw rested on his shoulder. Shane stepped back and quickly brushed the streaming blood out of his eyes. His blow traveled about eight inches and crashed. Sully zigzagged backward.

The gong rang in roars of applause.

Shane had one great advantage as a pugilist. His eyes were set deep in his head. The projecting forehead above, the high cheek-bones below, protected them. The blood stopped flowing above his eyes.

Silent Tim and Blinky Miller were in their element now. Not a move was wasted.

Blinky's hands worked rapidly over Shane's muscular legs, then his arms and shoulders, then up and down the back of his rope-like neck until his entire body was covered in the minute rest between rounds.

Another second swished a large towel in zigzag fashion, while Shane's enormous chest inhaled the freshly made air.

Silent Tim talked very low, his mouth close to Shane's ear. When the ten second bell rang, all made ready to clear the ring.

Shane looked across at his adversary.

Jack Gill leaned over Tim.

"Let me swing the towel next round."

"All right, Jack—thanks."

The gong rang. Shane decided to "play for his head."

He held his guard high and made no move until Sully moved. The audience screamed. Shane paid no attention. Each time the champion led he was beaten to the punch. Sully rushed while Shane was in mid-air. Shane fell from a right cross in a sickening crescendo of noise.

When he returned to his corner, Silent Tim said, "Work to his left, Shane—then go into your shell—don't let him outsmart you."

He smiled wearily at Jack Gill.

The champion was in Shane's corner before he had completely risen.

The fingers of the right hand stung from the impact, as his gloves swished with thudding pain. The champion crouched. Shane slammed him on the side of the head.

Unmindful of pain, the torturing sun on his naked body, and the fight-mad champion in front of him, he fought with grim set lips.

Shane countered two of Sully's now terrible drives with zipping uppercuts, and a jolt to the head.

They fell into a clinch. Shane's fists were every-where—now on Sully's jaws, now battering his body. The champion swayed under the terrible pounding.

"Keep away," Wilson shouted, "keep away! Good Lord, keep away!"

"Move in, Shane—remember Wichita," pleaded Jack Gill.

They broke free. Sully, his nose now split, his face

blood-bespattered, grinned for a brief second. Then his body became taut, lightning quick, to meet an even more terrible attack.

Torpedo Jones, watching, alert as a panther stalking his prey, moved his shoulders at each impact.

Their heads were now together. A looping right caught Shane on the temple. He staggered back and fell into a clinch before Sully could get set for a finishing blow.

In a wild flurry, Sully slipped and fell across the second rope of the ring. Shane, attacking with furious speed, stepped back until Sully was balanced. A thunderous roar followed the sudden act of courtesy in the midst of the mauling pain. Before it subsided, Sully was inside Shane's guard.

Standing flat-footed, his left as a jaw-protector, by some miraculous movement, Shane "tied Sully into knots" and left him helpless. The referee broke them.

They now began to counter.

Shane shifted suddenly. Toe to toe, they traded rights. Shane's left foot moved. Sully missed. Shane landed. Sully went back, his guard down.

They worked in different positions and stood waiting for counter punches at the bell.

"It's anybody's fight," Bangor Lang said to his companion.

Joe Slack's eyes were more narrow now. He was living over again the days of his vanished glory.

He nudged the fat man.

"These men were babies when I was in there," he said.

"Yeap—it's funny—babies then—think of it."

Shane's broad back glistened with water.

"For a man hittin' ghosts—he's landin' pretty often," said Jeremiah Dodge. "That Gill's nobody's fool either."

Joe Slack did not hear. He stared at the ring.

Shane advanced at the bell, slightly crouched, his left shoulder drawn up to protect his jaw from Sully's murderous right.

Sully was on his toes, his left feinting, his right ready for an attack.

He sprang in, but missed. Shane caught him going back and rocked him dizzily. With rapid brain, Sully maneuvered himself out of danger.

"He's not a champion for nothin'," said Jeremiah Dodge.

"They never are," commented Joe Slack, as Sully threw a thudding right against Shane's jaw. His entire body shook.

He fell for a split second on the ropes, dizzy with defeat had he been a lesser man. The kill in sight, Sully crashed in, snapping lefts and rights.

The audience stood screaming. A mad moment followed, when swift as an angry leopard leaping, Shane met Sully's attack. The amphitheatre was soon stunned into silence.

Uncountable blows, the neighbors of death, followed.

"He's zoomin' them now," screamed the fat man.

"Shut up, will you?" snapped Joe Slack.

Sully stepped back. Shane moved in.

In the number of blows landed with terrible and thudding accuracy, the next minute was unsurpassed in all the mad and bloody history of the ring.

Two men who could have stood against any other two of all time were whaling away at the summit of their mighty careers.

Jack Gill watched, like a runner ready to spring at the gong.

Each sensed a climax. They must withstand each other's blows without breaking. The champion dared not break ground under the withering bombardment of leather. Neither did Shane. It was such a moment that he who hesitated ever so briefly, unless it were for an overwhelming advantage, would know in his heart that, barring his delivering an accidental knockout, he was ultimately and forever defeated.

It was the final test. Each brain, each heart, every nerve and sinew of each was bent on the other's destruction. Mingled with hope of victory was the hatred engendered in former vicious fights. It was no longer the business of the two mightiest bruisers on earth battling for the greatest of pugilistic goals. It was something more—the epic struggle of young giants in the twilight of a weakened civilization. "I slugged Jerry Wayne crazy—I'll do the same for Rory." The words had once been ripped from Sully by Silent Tim Haney's taunts. Vivid as lightning, they were burned in Shane's brain.

Zip, zip, went their blows in close.

Silent Tim whispered to Jack Gill.

Shane shot an uppercut. Seeing it would miss and

expose him to Sully's attack, he stopped it in mid-air by a tremendous effort of will. His fist crashed on top of Sully's head.

The blow was forceful enough to loosen the brain in the champion's head. His knees sagged. His attack was, if possible, more vicious.

Without missing, as regular as maniacs pounding at a drum, each landed time and time again. One had to go to the canvas if sheer strength and fury would put him there. Brains and bodies trained for years in masterful coördination were giving all they had. Blows whistled like sharp winds. Each instinctively felt that hard blows, and not science, would win.

Sully's manager had a tense expression.

Blinky Miller's hands grasped the projecting edge of the ring. Like Gill, he was hunched over, ready to jump between the ropes at the gong.

"Rory's a great fighter," the fat man panted.

"They're both great," admitted Joe Slack.

The merciful gong ended the round.

Water splashed furiously on the determined gladiators. Silent Tim held a sponge at the back of Shane's head. Blinky Miller put smelling salts to his nose. Shane brushed it aside.

Typewriters clicker furiously. An airplane, droning unseen, slid a long shadow of wings across the ring.

Silent Tim whispered, "God's in your corner, lad, and me, and Jack and Blinky."

XXXII

Intent on the ring, forgetful of a half million profit in promoting the fight, Daniel Muldowney sat in the third row.

Shane shook his head furiously as the gong clanged.

Both men advanced swiftly and set a terrible pace. Shane's face twitched each time Sully landed a right. As they feinted and watched for openings, their feet could be heard shuffling over the hot canvas floor. The champion missed a right. It whizzed by the spot where Shane's jaw had been a second before. He tried again and missed. As he worked in close, Shane pounded Sully's kidneys. Each blow was like the explosion of a gun. Welts formed above them.

"It'll go the limit," Wilson whispered to the chief second.

The champion straightened Shane with a left upper-cut that rattled his teeth. They now volleyed rights and lefts to face and body and grunted as they landed. Shane staggered backward from a right. It was only for an instant. The crowd screamed to the champion, "You got him!" The champion leaped forward. Shane's body went rigid to meet the attack. It was like charging a stone wall. With hands that flailed oblivion, Shane made Sully retreat.

Soggy gloves ripped by soggy gloves. Their mus-

cular bodies writhed and reeled under the burning sun.
They slugged desperately in a neutral corner.

The champion started a blow. He was unable to
stop it when the gong rang. Shane dodged. The mo-
mentum of the blow threw Sully across the ropes.
Shane hurried to his corner with the hope of getting a
few seconds more rest than his antagonist.

"Have him go in his shell this round, Tim," advised
Gill.

Shane was in the champion's corner before the echo
of the gong died away. His arms were close to his
sides, his face buried in his gloves, his eyes peering
through. His body weaved like the upper end of a
rattler being teased.

Sully might have stared at a ghost on a country road.
He began to step back. Shane let loose suddenly.
Caught unawares with such savagery, the champion
retreated, his flying gloves bouncing from Shane's
weaving body.

Successfully dodging or blocking the terrible right,
Shane attacked with four perfectly timed blows, two
in the solar plexus, a right and left to Sully's jaws.

As though his feet had been shot from under him,
the champion went to his knees. Before he dropped,
Shane whipped another right to his jaw. Sully rolled
over twice. Roars of applause followed. Shane missed.
Sully jumped to his feet. Shane charged.

"There goes Roarin' Rory," shouted Hot and Cold
Daily.

Sully clinched against the ropes. The sweating referee, his white shirt blood-bespattered, loosened the

tangle of their powerful arms. The battering became more terrible. Their heads crashed together. Blood drooled from their mouths. They danced furiously for a second under the rigadoo of pain. The sun-scorched enclosure was again hushed into silence for a second.

"Oh, my God," panted Jeremiah Dodge, "my God, my God," and slumped in his seat.

Joe Slack glanced hurriedly at him. "Don't faint now," he sneered.

Shane dodged low. A ripping right landed on top of his head. The pain shooting to his shoulder blades touched him with madness. He crashed three powerful rights in a clinch. . . . "My God, he'll break him in two," yelled Jeremiah Dodge.

"He don't break so easy," snapped Joe Slack.

The sun scurried behind a cloud. The glaring outline of the ring was soft for a second. The voices of the mob died down in the presence of the fury that followed. Blinky Miller gripped the ring-post until his hands ached. Silent Tim mumbled to Jack Gill. Al Wilson twisted a towel and looked at Sully's chief second. A haze enveloped the fighters. They were tangled as the gong rang. The referee pried them apart.

"What round is it?" one reporter asked another.

"I don't know," was the answer, "the eleventh maybe."

It was the thirteenth.

Seconds and managers encouraged their fighters.

"Get him under the heart with your right—you got him goin'," said Wilson.

Sully's chest heaved up and down. He said nothing.

In the fourteenth, Shane worked his famous trick. Now feinting Sully to lead a straight right, he started one at the same time and moved his left foot a few inches.

Sully's right missed. Shane's landed. Sully went down for nine. He stretched out in a crucified position, the blazing sun in his eyes.

Screaming and gesticulating, the audience rose.

"Down, down," yelled many.

The gong rang. He was dragged to his corner.

The last round was coming up. The audience moved forward on their seats, numbed into silence.

The bell sounded.

The gloves of the fighters touched. They began to circle. A fusillade of leather followed. To save himself, the champion worked in close. A vicious right caught him under the heart. He grunted. His head fell on Shane's shoulder. He clung until it cleared, then squared for action.

Shane pushed his gloves aside. The gesture infuriated Sully. He lashed in.

An insect flew between the fighters. Caught on Shane's glove, it was smashed against Sully's forehead. The champion pounded Shane's sides. A hard left swished across his jaw.

Sully clinched.

The referee broke them.

He threw a whizzing right. Shane caught it in the air. The champion lambasted furiously.

Shane began a circling right. Sully moved away. Again Shane started the blow. Sully clinched.

Over Shane's shoulder, he saw Wilson's signal. "A minute to go."

As they broke, two rights were started. Sully's glove tore the skin from Shane's cheek as it whizzed over his shoulder.

Shane's left foot moved. Every muscle quivering with the fury of snakes on a griddle, Shane landed. The blow fractured Sully's chin. He staggered back, his hands dropping. Shane chopped with furious rights and lefts. Blood and water swished from his gloves as they hit their target.

Touched with the enormous madness of the scene, the huge audience was once more a punch-bowl of silence.

Sully staggered and rallied. His relentless antagonist moved in.

Two terrible rights crossed. One missed. The other landed.

A howl as of many winds started.

"Get up, Rory," a voice roared from a far seat.

The audience rose.

"Be seated." The words came from a gigantic megaphone.

"It's not Rory," snapped Hot and Cold Daily.

Sully squirmed and lay still.

At the count of ten he was dragged to his corner.

"Ladies and gentlemen," came the announcement, "the new Heavyweight Champion of the World."

The ring swarmed with people.

The police entered, "Clear the way—let 'em out."

Above the clamor could be heard, "Say a few words in the microphone, Mr. Rory."

The bulbs of photographers' cameras snapped on the scene.

During the mêlée, Sully's chief second came across Blinky Miller.

"You rat—I'll take that five grand outta your hide."

"G'wan and look after Sully."

Daily's story written and telephoned, he called, "Here boy, take this typewriter. I'll be in Rory's suite at the Royal—now don't forget." He said to another reporter, as Berniece joined him, "Take her with you."

The police made way for him as he followed Shane and his contingent from the ring.

"Take him, Blinky," Silent Tim commanded. Cheeks hollow and eyes tired from the strain of the battle, Shane's hands were still taped. A wound was above his eye; an abrasion was at the edge of his jaw, where Sully's blows had torn the unshaven hair away.

As in the ring, his lips were still tight pressed.

Blinky stripped him quickly and placed him under a shower, where two muscular men in bathing suits waited.

"Hold your hands out, Champ," Blinky said.

As the water touched the victorious fighter's shoulders, Blinky removed the tape, and rubbed the hands with satisfaction.

"Every knuckle in place, Champ."

The muscular men place Shane on a rubbing table. Blinky watched every movement.

In another room, a group of men talked the fight over.

"The boy has a heart of oak," said Daniel Muldowney.

"I knew he had Sully after that first round, eh, Tim," put in Jack Gill.

"It was a scorcher— I lived nine years in that three minutes." Silent Tim shook his head as if to drive away an evil memory.

"When he got Sully under the heart in the fourteenth—that was the wallop—he got me that way and I didn't know where I was till the fight was over." Bangor Lang was now heavier. "I'll see how he's comin'."

Shane smiled wearily, "Hello, Bangor."

Lang ignored the greeting. "Feeling all right, kid?" he asked, and continued, "That was a battle—Sully can sure as hell take it."

"And give it, Bangor," said Shane.

"Yep, how'd you ever figure he was a sucker for a right? I tried that on him and he damn near knocked my head out of the ring."

"I had to try something," returned Shane.

Jack Gill came in.

"Lord, Mick, I'd of fought the semi-windup for nothin' if Buck Logan could of seen you in there with Sully. I'll bet the old boy tried to get out of his coffin— I nearly had heart failure a dozen times—but I won ten grand—and you had to do all the fightin'."

"I'd go in there again to win money for you, Jack— remember Wichita?"

"I'll say so, Shane, remember Gunner Maley—poor devil. I saw him in Chicago—he was on his heels, walkin' up and down North Clark Street punchin' shadows. It won't be long now—he'll be with Jerry Wayne."

"Yeap," Lang acquiesced, "he was one of those fellows who always wanted to take a couple on the chin to give one. Too bad!"

Shane's mind was on Jerry Wayne. He became silent.

"Fight make you drowsy?" asked Jack Gill.

"A little, Jack."

Blinky patted Shane's arm.

"Come, Champ, we'll get you into your rags."

"Blinky won ten grand too, Jack," Shane smiled.

"That's more'n he ever won in the ring." Gill winked at Shane.

"Who?" snapped Blinky. "I could lick the both of you—in my day."

"I bet the dough in his name," Shane said to Gill.

"It's just like the sucker—he ain't happy unless he's doin' somethin' for someone—he'd even loan Sully dough."

"Well, you're set for life now, Shane—a million's not hard to take," said Bangor Lang.

"He earned it, Bangor," said Jack Gill.

A crowd still waited to watch the champion emerge. Newsboys cried, "Rory wins heavyweight title."

They were hardly in the hotel when the clerk announced a gentleman to see Mr. Daily.

"Send him up."

Daily opened the door. The reporter and another man stepped in followed by Berniece.

Shane watched the door. Peter Lund and Lyndal entered. Shane hurried to her. Silent Tim stared in surprise. Lang and Gill exchanged glances.

"Not bad," murmured Gill.

"Not at all," from Lang.

Shrewd in the ways of women, Gill said to Lang, "She's no pick-up," as she stepped close to Shane.

"Did you see the fight?" he asked bashfully.

"Yes."

"You brought me luck," he smiled.

"You needed it," grunted Old Peter.

"Why, you're all bruised," Lyndal looked at his eye.

"Yes, Babe, it's not ping-pong in there," Old Peter again grunted, before Hot and Cold Daily could introduce them.

"What's all this?" Silent Tim Haney frowned at Shane.

"What would you think?" cut in Hot and Cold Daily. "She's not challengin' him for the next fight."

"Well, well," Silent Tim looked at Daily, "did you do this?"

"Me and God," answered Daily.

"You would blame it on God," snapped Tim.

Shane put an arm about his irate manager.

"Listen, Tim," he said. "I'm retirin' in favor of Torpedo Jones. If Sully wants the championship he can fight him for it."

"But Torpedo's licked him already," exclaimed Tim, nonplused.

"That's Sully's business—he made me eat dirt."

"But that's foolish," said Daniel Muldowney.

"Sure it's foolish," shouted Tim.

"Maybe so, but a million's enough, besides—" he looked at Lyndal, "I just wanted to prove that I wouldn't run when the locusts came, either."

"Is your mind failin'?" Tim asked in alarm.

Lyndal answered, "No, it's a secret we have between us."

"All right, to hell with it. I had a champion for a minute." Tim scowled at Daily.

"Yeah—you and poor Daniel Muldowney—you're both down to your last few million."

"But it's wrong, Daily—it's not practical—it's the act of a poet." In Tim's voice was a sob. "It's crazy—why he can make several million more."

"No, Tim, that's what Jerry Wayne thought," Shane put in. "I'm through."

Lyndal looked from Shane to his manager.

"He's right, Tim," put in Bangor Lang. "He'd be no good to you anyhow, feeling the way he does."

"It's still looney," objected Tim. "It's the thought of a madman."

"Don't be silly," Hot and Cold Daily clapped his hands. "It's a great story—Champion retires in favor of Torpedo Jones on night of great victory. A Negro given championship first time in history of the world. Jones and Rory once road kids together. Champ to marry heiress . . . they'll eat it up."

Hot and Cold Daily snapped his fingers and smiled with satisfaction.

"Pose for a picture."

Berniece crossed to Lyndal. "I'm happy for you," she said.

"Thank you so much." Arm in arm the girls stepped aside.

"Mr. Daily and I have been sweethearts a long time," Berniece confided—"he's awfully fond of Shane—we just know you'll be happy."

Hot and Cold Daily could be heard telephoning his story.

"I'll still go with you, won't I, Champ?" asked Blinky Miller.

"Sure thing, Blinky," said Shane.

Turning from the telephone, Daily took Berniece's arm, "Let's all go to the Tavern—that story'll knock 'em dead."

"All right," agreed Shane, "let's go." Humming,

> "Every painted lady
> Is some lonely mother's baby—
> But on Broadway
> She's a wild, wild rose."

Daily, still holding Berniece's arm, followed the crowd slowly.

"Brace up, Berniece, it's all in the game. If you win, you lose."

"I know," responded Berniece.